My Friend

My Pain

By:

MARGIE HEART

Table of Contents

Chapter 1

Teressa could not quite understand it. Her marriage was deteriorating right in front of her eyes. Her husband had changed completely. She could not cope with him anymore.

She sat down on her bed with her eyes clouded with tears; she let them stream down her face and cried until the pain in her chest subsided. She felt better and began packing her bags. She saw no reason she should keep on staying with Patrick who no longer loved her.

After packing she went through every room saying goodbye to her house. It was the last time for her to set foot in a house that she had helped furnish with love and adoration. Finally, she picked up her suitcase and went out locking the door after her.

She decided to go and live with her friend Linda. Her marriage had lasted six painful months. When she got to her car, she could not bring herself to look at the house because of the pain in her heart. Their house was so beautiful that it attracted passersby. Having to leave all that, broke her heart. But it had to be done for her sanity and safety.

Finally, she entered her car and drove away with a lump deep down her throat. She could not even concentrate on the traffic ahead of her. Luckily, it was daytime, and traffic was minimal, so no harm was done there. She kept on thinking about Patrick. Teressa loved Patrick so much that even when their marriage was deteriorating, she could not bring herself to hate him.

Linda could not believe her eyes.

"Is that her or am I dreaming?" she asked herself.

Ever since Teressa got married these two friends had never visited one another. As Linda sees Teressa's car she was surprised. They had been best friends since high school.

"Yes, that is her. But she is thin. I wonder why." Linda mused. She was surprised when her friend descended from the car. She could not stand by the window anymore and ran outside to meet her friend.

Teressa also ran to meet her friend. She threw the suitcase down and hugged Linda extremely hard. Linda was even more surprised at how thin her friend felt in her arms. They stood like that for some time without uttering any words to each other because of the joy they felt.

Lastly, Linda found the strength to say "let's go inside darling" as she picked up the forgotten suitcase.

They went inside the house holding hands.

"Hello Terry, my friend" greeted Linda.

"Hello Li sweetheart. It has been a long time. I missed you so much. Why didn't you write to me or even call me?" said Terry ending with a question.

"Sorry Terry I have been so busy at work, and I could not find the time. Tell me dear, you look so slim and worried; what is going on, is everything okay between you and Patrick?"

Linda could not wait any longer to ask the questions that were on her mind. Instead of answering Teressa began to cry. Linda could tell that nothing was good. Teressa was not someone who cries easily. If she cried it means things were really bad. Linda did not like the idea of Teressa leaving her job when she got married. She had tried to reason with her to no avail because Teressa thought it was a clever idea that she become a stay-at-home wife, have children, and take care of them, her household, and her husband.

Teressa cried and cried. Linda soothed her murmuring soft words to her. She finally stopped crying.

"Linda my friend, it is a long story. I cannot bring myself to say it now. What I want now is a long warm shower and rest. I will tell you later. I have not been sleeping well for a long time, and I feel so tired. I could fall asleep on my feet right now. Will you take me in for a few days, please? "After this long speech, Linda felt sorry for her friend. She had not imagined her to be having problems in her marriage.

"Yes darling. You know this is your home anytime. Use your usual room and take your time resting. Dinner will be ready at 7 pm so you have plenty of time to rest. See you later."

Linda thought it was wise not to pursue the subject of her friend's sullenness. Teressa will tell her when she is ready to talk even though she was eager to know what happened. Teressa picked up her suitcase and went upstairs to her old bedroom. The bedroom was facing the river that was close by. It was her favorite room. She had painted it sky blue and put pictures of the moon and the stars on the wall.

The furniture was a mixture of sky blue and white. There was a fitted wardrobe with mirrored doors, a double bed, a white dressing table, and a full-length mirror at the foot of the bed. The room was simple but elegant. This room made her feel at peace. She felt like she was breathing new fresh air with the hope of a new fresh life.

"It feels good to be in familiar surroundings after being in hell." She thought. Teressa thought her new home was hell. Hell, because it lacked the warmth and love that she had sought in Patrick. Hell, because there was no laughter and happiness she used to enjoy during the first weeks of her marriage. Patrick had turned a fun-loving home into hell.

She took her bath in the bathroom that was next to her room. Afterward, she decided to take a nap before she unpacked her suitcase. She slept for the whole 2 hours.

All the tiredness from the sleepless nights came and she slept like a baby, a dreamless sleep. When she woke up, she unpacked her suitcase, got changed, and decided to wear deep makeup for that day for a change. She was trying to retain a bit of color on her face.

All along Linda was preparing her friend's favorite food for them. She kept on wondering what was troubling her friend so much. She wondered what made Teressa run away from her marital home if she ran away. Her friend was always smiling and laughing but she came back a totally different person and looked miserable with no smile on her face at all.

"Terry to cry, that's something," she thought. Teressa could not cry even when her mother passed away. Her eyes were dryer than usual. That was the first day Linda had seen Teressa crying. While deep in thought she heard,

"HMMM smells good! What is in those pots that is making my stomach grumble?" Teressa had not realized how hungry she was. She was welcomed by the delicious smell of food as she descended the stairs.

Linda was making the finishing touches on the dinner table. She turned to look at her friend.

"At least there is a change," she thought to herself.

"Hey Terry, welcome back. You look much better darling. I was about to call you to come down for dinner. Come sit and let us see who is going to win this battle between food and us!" said Linda ending with a joke. Teressa laughed for the first time in months and it felt good.

"I had not realized how hungry I am. Obviously, I am going to win. You have not left your old habits, Linda. Always jokes and jokes. I missed them"

They ate in silence. Terry felt better and almost her old self. She was ready to tell her friend what happened to her marriage.

"Linda, my friend, I never knew that marrying Patrick would be like this." began Teressa. She thought that confiding in someone will reduce the weight on her shoulders. It was time for Linda to hear the full story about her friend.

"Yes Terry, I have been wondering all day what could be wrong. You are not the Teressa I know. I could sense that something is not right. What is it?" encouraged Linda.

"Li I could not 't visits you. Pat turned out to be a violent person I have ever known. He did not allow me to visit anyone let alone you, my friend. I wish I had not left my job and married him. He was so sweet at the beginning ...."

"Terry, get straight to the point. Do not beat about the bushes. I want to know everything from the beginning" Linda cut her friend short in mid-sentence.

"Well, this is what happened. Two weeks after marriage I discovered that the agent that Patrick was working for was a lie. Instead, it was a gang of robbers, pat was not the manager he claimed to be. Instead, the agent was a secret gang of robbers that he belonged to. One day I found a letter in the drawer that was from his boss.

The leader was complaining that Patrick was not attending their meetings. Those meetings were happening after we got married. It also stated that he was not doing his job and that was he expecting to get paid for not working. He was instructed to go and rob a house in a street that I do not even think exists by that name.

When I asked him about it, he got so angry and that is when everything changed. He beat me up that I ended up having a blue eye. From that day he would go and come back at midnight. At times he would wake me up for silly questions and beat me up for nothing." It was all tears on both their faces. Linda found it hard to believe that this was the Patrick that she knew.

"Patrick a robber! It's hard to believe it. After the discovery why didn't you report him? Were you intending to leave him? What happened?" Linda asked when Terry had gone silent for a while. She asked the questions that were in her mind from the beginning of the tell tale.

Teressa said "No, I was not intending on leaving him. I only wanted to know as his wife. You see I believe there is no need to keep secrets from each other when we are married. I love him and I would not have left him for his bad job. I would have convinced him to change professions instead.

"From that time, he went to sleep in a different bedroom and whenever we are together, it was arguments and beatings. Linda, it was like leaving in hell."

Linda felt sorry for her friend. "That's why she is so thin," Linda thought.

"Hmm, so Pat was dangerous. He could have killed you one day," says Linda.

"Yeah, I was afraid of that. One day he just changed and became so lovely. He became the Patrick I fell in love with. He talked and laughed and even called me darling. This happened 2 months ago. We even shared a bed that night. But after that night he became worse and more violent." By this time Terry was sobbing hard remembering the terrible time she has been through.

Linda waited for her friend to calm down before saying, "That is incredibly sad and surprising. What had made him change suddenly?"

"As it had been some time since we were intimate, I was no longer on the pill. When he asked me afterward, I told him so and he became so furious that he could have killed me there and then."

"Why?" Asked Linda.

"He said what if I fall pregnant? He is not prepared to be a father yet. It means that I did this on purpose so that I can tie him down permanently. Expenses of parenthood are too high, and I said I can go back to work he said that is out of the question. Linda that was a horrible argument. He no longer spoke to me, and it became worse than before.

"I was beaten every day. Using cords, belts, shoes oohhh anything that was within his reach. So today when I got a small opportunity, I thought it wise to leave the dreadful place and its biting owner," ended Teressa with a sigh of relief for having confided to someone.

Linda was not pleased with her friend's choice. "But Terry I do not think that was wise. Remember you contributed to that house being built and furnished it with your money, love, and time. What are you going to do about that?" she ended with a question.

"Nothing. I do not even want a single cent from him. If I ask for anything I will be opening doors for him to kill me. Let him enjoy the comfort. It is only material things. God will bless me with more." Said Teressa not even wanting to think about talking to Patrick let alone ask for a divorce or a share of her property.

"You are right my friend. Well, I have no comments! Only to say thank God you are still here. Remember your pain is also my pain. You should have told me as soon as all this began. I would have done something about it," Says Linda.

"That was impossible. Like I said before, I was not permitted to leave the premises or even use the telephone," said Teressa with pain in her heart.

"That is too bad. Anyway, I am here now. With me no more pain. Cheer up sweetie. No Patrick is going to trouble you anymore here. This is your home from long back." Linda said trying to cheer her friend up.

All of a sudden Teressa started to panic.

"What if he follows me here? I do not think I am safe anywhere in this world!" said Teressa when she suddenly remembered that she had not thought that he will come looking for her here. All of a sudden, she does not feel safe anymore. She does not feel at peace anymore.

"With Jesus Christ guiding you, yes you are fine here. For now, try to forget him my friend. I will make sure he does not get to you. Anyway, what are your future plans?" Linda ended with a question.

"None at the moment. I will have thought better tomorrow. Let us go wash plates. They have gone dry. Thanks for a delightful meal. I had not realized how hungry I was. Linda, you were always a darling and always will be. Thank you for listening to me." Terry felt better after confiding in her friend.

They cleared the table and took the dishes to the kitchen for washing up.

"Wow what a day and what an evening. It is nice to be with you again. Feel at home as this is your home too. Jim will be so pleased to see you," says Linda.

"Oh, how silly of me. Talking of Jim how is he?" asked Terry. Jim was Linda's boyfriend. They chatted about different things that happened in their lives updating each other about what has happened in each other's absence.

Linda felt tired and it was really late. She wanted to go to bed to prepare for the next day as she was going to work. She said, "Welcome home and Good night sweetie."

"Thank you and night hun. It feels so good to be home again," Teressa said as she headed to her bedroom. She also felt exhausted and almost in better health. This house Linda and herself had contributed some money to buy it together. It had cost them fifty thousand dollars and they had paid half each, the house was a four bedrooms house with a kitchen dining room, a kitchen, and a veranda overlooking the road. Two of the bedrooms were en-suites and these were theirs and the other two were guest bedrooms. At the back, there was a swimming pool and a tennis court. In front, there was a lawn and flowers. It was an incredibly beautiful house.

There was a driveway that led from the gates to the parking lot, The river was a short distance away separating their house and their neighbor's house. It was indeed a breath-taking beautiful home. The decorations inside were outstanding. Just imagine it being decorated and furnished by two experts!

Before Teressa got married, she was working as a sales executive for a large clothing factory in town and the salary was really good making her afford anything she wanted. Linda was a private investigator and she also earned good money. To both of them, money was not a problem.

They had agreed that whenever they get married, they will not sell their property. Instead, they will use it as a family home, a place for them to go to as they were both orphans and did not have any other family home.

Chapter 2

When Patrick arrived home, he was greeted by a cold place with no fires lit or any lights on. He was somehow glad and sad at the same time; He had left the house early in the morning with an appointment with his boss. He could not concentrate on his work anymore.

Teressa frightened him. He used violence to hide his fear. Ever since she saw his letter, he was afraid that she might tell someone about his secret job which could result in him being arrested. He loved his wife. He was afraid of losing her. He had intended to keep his job a secret from her until he resigns and find a descent honest job.

That day when he left in the morning, he was going to talk to his boss about it. His boss had agreed to let him go on condition that he will not tell anyone about the dealings of their secret agent job. Patrick had agreed and intended to keep his promise because he did not want to lose the life of his family.

When he headed home, he was intending to apologize to his wife and tell her the good news. He knew that his ill-treatment of her could lead her to tell her friend Linda and he will be in massive trouble. So, he stopped her from calling Linda, from going anywhere even shopping because he was afraid that she might escape. He somehow managed to keep her in by locking her in the house and making sure there are no spare keys left in the house.

That morning he was so preoccupied that he forgot to lock the doors which is why Teressa managed to escape. To Patrick's surprise, when he arrived home Teressa's car was missing. At first, he thought it must have been stolen. So, he rushed in to ask her if she had heard or seen anything, another surprise was that when he got to the door, it was not locked. He rushed in and called Teressa's name and was greeted with silence. He panicked thinking that maybe something had happened to her. He feared that he might have hurt her so bad that she is lying down dying or dead. Or she could have taken her own life. Fear gripped him and he felt weak at his knees. He had tried to be so careful so as not to hurt her too much. He just wanted to inflict enough pain that will inflict fear in her so that she does not report him. He mustered the courage to walk around the house and look for her.

But signs of doors unlocked and car missing told him she is okay and might have run away. He went into the master's bedroom that Teressa used and found out that one suitcase and some of her clothes were missing. He knew instantly without a doubt that she had escaped. Her documents were gone. All the draws that had her belongings were empty except the ones that had his belongings.

"Ohh no she really is gone. I am sorry Terry my wife. I was not ill-treating you because I wanted to. It hurt me all the times I hurt you. Why did you leave me at a time when I was coming home to fix things? Why did you leave me so suddenly?!" cried Patrick. He had not realized how much he loved his wife until that morning.

Yes, he missed her cooking. Not eating was because he was afraid. Of what? Even he did not know. Or so he thought. He came to realize that he was afraid to connect with her more because her food was delicious. He was afraid that enjoying her food will make him give her nice comments and that will make it difficult for him to actually maintain the horrible behavior that he was trying so hard to maintain. He sat on the bed and cried.

"This house is incredibly beautiful, and this is because of her. Now with her gone how am I supposed to enjoy its comfort?" thought Patrick. "I love her. I have to find her wherever she has gone to. Yes, I have to find her and with confidence I know I can find her." With that decision, he felt better and decided to prepare some food and go to bed early to prepare to begin his search for her the next day.

"Tomorrow I will look for my wife and a decent job," He thought. He went to the kitchen to prepare the food but found that his appetite was gone and just went to sleep on an empty stomach.

Early the following day at around five in the morning he woke up with a start. He was dreaming of his wife and himself making passionate love. He was enjoying himself and Teressa was even her old self. He was far from climaxing when he raised his head and saw his former boss standing by the dressing table and he was pointing a knife at them. He demanded that Patrick get up and sit on the dressing table chair, which Patrick did. He motioned to him that if they scream, he is going to kill them. His boss then moved towards the bed to where

Teressa was. That is when Patrick jumped to act, and he woke up.

He recalled the dream and wondered what it meant. He decided it must be his subconscious mind playing with him for missing his wife and having left a terrible job. He got off the bed and went to shower. He brushed his teeth and felt clean. He put on smart clothes and made up his bed.

The first thing he thought of starting his search was to call Linda. He knew that Linda's place was the first place his wife could possibly go to as it was her former home. Afterward he will get a newspaper, look at the jobs section, and start applying for jobs.

He dialed Linda's number.

"Hello!" that was the voice on the other end of the call, Linda's voice.

"Hello!" replied Patrick in his deep throaty voice. "Sorry Linda did I wake you up?" he asked.

"No, I was already awake cleaning up my place. What can I do for you Pat? What makes you call me so early in the morning after such a long time I have not heard from you guys?" asked Linda.

"Sorry to disturb you. I have a problem. Yesterday when I got home in the evening Terry was missing. Is she at your place?" He asked with a pained heart.

"What? Terry missing! Are you sure Patrick?" Linda made her voice sound surprised.

"Yes Linda, she is missing. Does this mean she is not with you then? Do you have any idea where she might be?"

"She is not here, and I have no idea where she might be. Pat was everything okay with the two of you? How can she just be missing? Where is she? Are you guys pranking me or playing hide and seek with me? You know you cannot easily hide from me! When Terry is missing, you know it is my duty to look for her and make sure she is okay. I am her only closest person to family and I care deeply. Are you guys tricking me?" Asked Linda breathlessly one question after the other pretending to be in the dark.

When Teressa heard her friend shouting on the phone, she came downstairs to find out if everything was okay.

She listened to the conversation which turned out to be with her husband. Linda signaled her to be silent, and Teressa left her to manage Patrick.

"I am not tricking you, Linda. I am serious. Do you think I would joke like this? We had a slight misunderstanding and she got angry. Now her belongings and car are gone. I love my wife Linda and I am really worried. Please help me find her if you can." Patrick pleaded getting more worried now that he was told Teressa is not at Linda's house.

"Well, if you are serious, I am also serious. She is not here. What can we do Pat? I am worried. I hope your misunderstanding is not too serious that she could decide to take her own life. We have to find her soon Pat before it is too late." Replied Linda.

"Yes Linda. I do not know where else she could have gone. It is best I inform the police. I had hoped she will be at your place and we could talk and patch things up. Now I have no choice but to inform them in case I think she left but she was kidnapped!" Patrick felt like crying now when he thought of the possibility that she was kidnapped.

He was now thinking that maybe his former bosses pretended to let him go and yet deep down they did not want him gone and this was their way of keeping him. Kidnapping his wife would give them the power to bargain her for him to do another job. He got scared and felt pain in his heart.

"No! Wait to call the police. As I am a private detective let me do the investigations. I will ask my colleagues to help me. I will keep you informed, and you too keep your eyes and ears open." Linda convinced Patrick to keep the police out because she knew they will find them quickly and she did not know what Teressa wanted to be done. She wanted to talk to her first.

"Thank you for your support, Linda. I will do as you say. And please whenever you see my wife, tell her I love her very much and may she please come back home."

"Okay Pat, Bye now."

Patrick replied "Bye and thanks."

They hung up. Patrick did not know what to do next. Where he thought his wife was, apparently, she was not there. He thought it was better because her friend would give a hand in the search. He promised himself he will open his eyes very wide wherever he was walking and listen to people in case he eavesdrops on people talking about or to her. He decided that he was going to ask all her old friends and her former colleagues in case she decided to go and ask for her job back.

He went to buy a newspaper. He read the vacancies first as he was desperate to find out if there were any available jobs out there. Luck was on his side. There was an advert for a supervisor at the big hypermarket in town and the duties included supervision of workers, buying stock, and running the hypermarket. The applicant was asked to provide a detailed CV and certificates. He did not waste time. He has all the required qualifications. He took his car keys and documents and went to his car. Making sure he locked the door after him. He made his way to B & F Hypermarket.

Patrick had grown up in poverty. His parents were poor and they for a certain farmer who paid them peanuts. They could not afford to pay for school fees for their only son. Patrick helped around the farm. When he was 15 years old, he ran away from home and went to an urban town with no particular place to go. That is when he met a man who claimed to be Brother Jojo and he promised him a place to stay and said he will look after him.

In return Patrick had to join his workforce. That is how he joined the gang of robbers. After a while in the gang, he was paid. He then asked Brother Jojo for permission to go to school. Jojo agreed. One day he met a man from his homestead who found out what he was doing for a living. The man went to tell his parents who got angry and disowned him.

Patrick was disappointed and hurt. But there was nothing he could do because he did not want to work in the farm all his life. All he wanted was to create a better future for himself and at the right time remove himself from the life of crime. He went on to night school. Did his primary education, secondary education and then went on to do a management course in college using the robbery money to pay for his fees.

During all that time he had no committed relationship. He did not like the idea of falling in love because of his lifestyle he knew that no one will be safe in his life. When he completed his college education, he decided to make amends with his parents. But first he had to buy them gifts as an apology and tell them of his future plans.

He went to the most expensive clothes shop in town the Markels. When he arrived there, there was this beautiful woman who seemed to be talking to other staff members. She seemed to be giving them instructions. He got hooked. He could not take his eyes off her. The woman was beautiful and captivating. He fell head over heels in love for the first time and at first sight.

When Teressa turned to leave, she caught sight of this handsome breath-taking guy and was surprised to see him looking at her smiling. She nearly collapsed and she too fell in love at first sight. It felt like a fairy tale. Patrick greeted her, and bought the most expensive dress in the store. When leaving he asked for her number, and she could not refuse. That is how the friendship began.

It developed into a more intimate relationship which ended up being a marriage. Patrick had kept his job a secret and lied to her about what he does for a living. He was afraid that if he tells her, she will not want to be with him. All the while he continued to higher education until he got Bachelors' Degree in Business Management.

Instead of looking for a decent job there and then he wanted to quit his gangster lifestyle first so that he can have a good, pleasant safe life with his family. After marrying Teressa, he informed his parent who were happy for him but still made it clear that he could only go home when he quits his gangster lifestyle.

So now he rushed to B & F Hypermarket thinking in his mind how his parents will be thrilled that he has finally quit the gangster lifestyle and is going to live an honest life. He intended to go home to his parents over the weekend to tell them the good news. He arrived at the Hypermarket and requested to see the employer. He was shown to his office. He knocked on the door.

"Come in!" said someone inside.

"Please take a seat." instructed a man who had a name label written Edward Enders. Patrick sat down on the chair he was given.

"Good morning" greeted Mr. Enders.

"Good morning, sir" replied Patrick.

"How can I help you?" asked Mr. Enders.

"My name is Patrick Anderson. I came in response to the advert that you posted in the newspaper that states that you are looking for a supervisor. I am looking for a job and I have all the qualifications that you asked for" replied Patrick.

Mr. Enders looked at him in silence. He was regarding this guy who looked so handsome, was so polite and well mannered but seemed confident as well. From the first appearances, he looked at the part that he was looking for. But he had to ask to see the qualifications.

"Mhhhh, I see. Let me see your qualifications please?"

Patrick passed on his certificates and CV to Mr. Enders. He read them quickly. On paper, the man sounded really good and had all the qualifications. He wanted to hire him on the spot, but he had to be sure and had to follow the rules and regulations of employing someone in his company.

"You are 32 years old right?"

"*Yes sir*" replied Patrick.

"Are you married?"

"Yes sir."

"Do you have children?"

"Not yet sir"

"So that means you are a newly wed?" Mr. Enders asked smiling.

"Yes, sir I got married 6 months ago" replied Patrick thinking that the gentleman is nice.

Mr. Enders asked a lot more questions including the ones that wanted to know about his resting routines because he said that the job was very demanding and needed someone willing to work hard but also give themselves enough time to rest.

In the end, time had come to know if he had made an impression or not.

"Do you think you can manage a job?" Mr. Enders asked with a smile lingering on his lips.

"Yes sir" replied Patrick. "I have confidence that I can do the job to the best of my ability. I am capable of also managing myself and coping with the difficulties that the job offers.

"Fair enough. If you get the job, I will call you. I need to see a few more candidates and chose the best. I hope you understand. Please leave copies of your certificates at the reception.

"Thank you, sir." Patrick left feeling positive. He felt like he already got the job and could not wait to get that phone call. He went home to wait for the phone call.

In the evening around 5pm the long-awaited phone call came.

"Good day Mr. Anderson. This is Mr. Enders. Apologies for calling late. It has been a busy day as you can recall how many people were waiting to see me when you left." said Mr. Enders.

Patrick said "Thank you sir for calling me. I understand you are a busy man sir."

"Well, I was impressed with the way you presented yourself today including your qualifications. I would like to give you the opportunity to join my team. You got the job!" continued Mr. Enders.

Patrick wanted to jump with joy. He could not believe he has landed himself a respectable job. They continued to talk about salary terms, and what was expected of him. He was told to start the following day if he could as the company was desperate for an immediate start of the new appointee.

"Thank you very much sir" thanked Patrick pleasantry.

"Okay, Mr. Anderson. See you tomorrow," said Mr. Enders

Patrick felt like flying. He had never felt so joyful in his life. He wanted to share this joy with Teressa, but it was impossible. Thinking about his wife his joy diminished. He loved his wife so much and missed her badly. He decided to continue to go and see his parents at the weekend to tell them about his fortune and rebuild his relationship with them.

The following day he went to his new workplace. He was shown to his office and signed the paperwork. The duties had begun. He felt welcome at the Hypermarket. All staffs were lovely and welcoming. But he dreaded going home because his wife was not there, and it was the gloom of his days not knowing what to do and not having her to share what he did during the day.

On Saturday he went home to see his parents. He bought them presents. When he arrived, his father was in the garden and his mother doing her duties in the kitchen of the River family they were working for. The first person to see him was a small boy. He ran inside to tell his family about a stranger outside. The boy had never seen Patrick as he left before the boy was born.

Mr. River came outside as Patrick was descending from his car. He could not believe his eyes. This big guy looked like Anderson's son/ Patrick was surprised to see Mr. River had grown older and had grey hairs.

"Hello, young man" greeted Mr. River.

"Hello, Mr. River." Yes, the voice was that of the 15-year-old boy who left all those years ago.

"You can't tell it's me Pat" It was half a question half a statement. Mr. River grabbed Patrick's hand and shook it firmly with happiness. He was happy to see the respectable young man that the boy who used to be thin and shy had turned out to be.

"I am incredibly happy to see you, Pat. I thought you had ditched us. You have grown so big and look very respectable Pat. By the way, your father did tell me that he hears from you often. Ohh Pat, your mum said you are married. Where is your wife?"

"Mr. River is still a talkative man," thought Patrick. He just did not like the idea of being reminded about his wife whom he has not seen or heard of for four days.

"She was busy and couldn't come with me today" Patrick lied. "Where is mum and paps?" He asked.

"You haven't forgotten your old habits of calling your father Paps," laughed Mr. River. "I want us to surprise them. I will take you to my living room and tell them of a certain young man wanting to see them. I want to see if they can remember you" he said laughing and enjoying the moment. They went into the living room through the back door.

"Go on then. I want to see that too," encouraged Patrick.

Mr. River first went to collect Patrick's father in the garden, and they passed by to get Mrs. Anderson who was with Mrs. River in the kitchen. The Andersons were surprised who would come to see them who was unknown to Mr. River. When they entered the living room, they all stood motionless by the door. They could not believe their eyes. The man sitting there was too handsome to be him.

Patrick was wearing a navy blue suit with black shoes and a white shirt. He was dressed too smart for the 15-year-old they all knew.

"Pat, is that you son?" asked Mrs. Anderson doubtfully when she could find her voice.

"Yes, it's him sis Dolly!" laughed Mr. River. He used Patrick's mother's nickname.

"No Clive it can't be him," says Mrs. River. "Is it really you Patrick?" she too asked debating with her husband.

Patrick smiled broadly and said, "yes it's me mum, pap, and Mrs. River." His voice was soft and deep as they knew it when he was growing up and Mrs. River always envied and wished he were his son.

His parents rushed to his side. He stood up to meet them and welcomed them with open arms. They all cried and had so much they wanted to say to each other, but they could not say it in front of the Rivers.

"Sonny welcome back home. Ohh how we've missed you Ticky!" At last, his dad found his voice. He had been silent all along not believing that this young man standing in front of him is his son. He had never been so happy in his life like he has always been in time past. He called Patrick by his childhood name that he so loved calling him and this reminded Patrick of the past when he was young when his parents used to spoil him a lot. They might have been poor but, his parents gave him all the love he needed. And they made sure that he gets the essentials even though they could not afford to send him to the school that he wanted.

"Well, well well. Everyone is happy to see you Pat" said Mr. River after Patrick had greeted everyone. "Andersons, you can take the whole weekend off to spend and enjoy with your son," he ended. The Andersons thanked them and left. The Rivers envied them for having a wonderful son unlike them. They had a grandson, but he too was not comparable to Patrick even as a child.

The Anderson reached their cottage. All the questions they had for Patrick came tumbling out of their lips.

"Pat, son. I know that we could not afford to take you to school on the little money that we earned, but we brought you up with love and gave you everything that we could. What troubles us is why you left to join the aging of robbers. You should have stayed here and worked in the farm like us. Why son did you leave?" Asked his father.

"Pap, I thank you for the love, support, and devotion that you gave me. I appreciate that very much all my life. It is not because of you that I left. You did not fail me. I knew you did all you could. I just could not continue watching other children my age going to school while I did farm work. I could not stand the future working in the farm all my life for others including those children my age. I had to do something. I wanted to go to the city and look for a job. When I left I had nowhere particular to go.............." Patrick responded.

He told them about everything that happened to him and how he ended up being a part of a gang just to have a roof over his head, how once in he could not get out. He mentioned how he went to night school, college, and university. He told his parents about meeting Teressa and falling in love. He mentioned how the marriage was, and how he has now left the gang and got a decent job. He told them of his wish of having his wife back. He even told them that he wanted to come back home as a respectable man that they will be proud of and win their love all over again and also return the love that they gave him and the values about life.

"I love you mum and pap. I hope you forgive me for the wrong I have done and the pain I have caused you. I also wish God will forgive me and send Terry back to me," ended Patrick. His parents were silently listening, and they were in tears both of joy and sadness at hearing what their son went through.

His father said "Ticky I knew that one day you will come back home. It is a sad story you have told us, and we are deeply sorry that you went through all this. It's a shame that we could not protect you from the world's pains. The good thing is that it ends in happiness except for your missing wife. When she is ready for you, she will come back. Wish you good luck my son. I hope she will one day know what a good man you are." He took a sigh and continued.

"I just wish I had met my daughter-in-law that you speak so highly of. Of course, we forgive you sonny," ended his dad.

"Your dad is right Ticky. We knew you were a good boy. We were just disappointed at what happened, and we were hoping you will go back to being the special boy we raised. We prayed you would return home and remove us from the fire," added his mother who had been sobbing silently listening to her so's telltale with pain in her heart. She tried to end with a joke. Just being glad her son came out of this an improved man.

"Talking of removing you from the fire, it reminds me I have my bags in the car and your presents," said Patrick who had forgotten about them when he saw his parents.

Together they left and went to fetch them. They came back to the cottage. Patrick gave his parents their presents. There were other small presents he had brought for the Rivers and he asked his father to go and give them. He had a special present that he had wished to give to his parents ever since he was a child. He had kept it to himself all the time.

"This is the best opportunity for me to tell them," He thought.

"Mum, Pap I have got a special present that I want to give you," he began. "I had wished to give you since I was a small boy, and I knew God will help me make my dream come true one day."

"What is it Ticky?" his parents asked at the same time, and they all laughed at that.

"You guys have been in a farm all your lives and I wanted to buy you a farm of your own. I wanted you to stop working in someone else's farm and someone else's kitchen but have other work in yours. I have somehow bought it for you" His parents were dumbfounded. They could not believe that they heard him correctly. They looked at him like they are seeing him for the first time that day.

"Paps, I want you to tell Mr. River you are leaving tomorrow when you take their presents and apologize for the sudden departure. Please do not tell him where you are going. I will take care of that." He asked his father.

"My son, my son I do not know what to say. I cannot think. How do I thank you? I think God sent me an Angel from heaven. Or I will wake up from a dream! I cannot believe this is really you doing this for us! You have no idea how much your dad and I wished we could have a farm of our own. Thank you so much. May God bless you all your life my boy!" said his mum full of joy kissing him all over and hugging him countless times on the cheeks.

"It's my pleasure mum to see you happy and your dream coming through." Patrick could not stop smiling; his cheeks were hurting from smiling too much.

"Your mum has already said everything Ticky. May the Lord take care of you always. Thank you so much, Ticky. We love you very much. I will do as you say when I take their presents." His father added as he ended with pride.

This present took away all the years of pain and hurt that they felt when their son left which became worse when they heard that he had joined a gang of robbers. They could tell he was trying his best to make amends and this gave them warmth in their hearts.

"Okay, dear parents. Let me change and go see the surrounding. I long for my childhood memories. I want to see what changes happened while I was away. See you later." Said Patrick jumping about and feeling like a little kid like he used to whenever he was with his parents, and they were having fun.

He left his parent beaming with joy and pride. In his mind, he did not care about the surroundings or the memories. He wanted to be alone to think about his wife undisturbed. He was wondering how proud she would have been of him. He could almost see the pleasure on her face and nearly smiled at himself. It was sad how much he missed him.

During the evening his father did as Patrick had asked, The Rivers were hurt but they were happy for the Andersons. They slept. The following morning the Andersons woke up early and packed up their belongings. They went to bid farewell to the Rivers.

Mr. River asked Patrick "Where are you taking your parents Patrick? I hope it is a wonderful place."

"I've bought a farm for them, and I want them to become full-time farmers in their own space," Patrick replied proudly.

"That is great and that is being a good boy. Good luck and bye now," said the Rivers who did not like the idea of losing their workers to a farm that sounded better than theirs when Patrick was telling them about it.

Patrick had not told his parents where the farm was or what it looked like, the farm was along Glees road. The main motorway that led to the city. It was one of the best farms in the country. When they arrived at the farm, they entered the gates. His parents had no idea what lay in front of them, and they waited in anticipation. As they entered another gate that led to the house, they could not believe their eyes.

"But Ticky, how come you did not tell us that you are taking us to a palace? We are not prepared to meet the King!" said his father jokingly who was so surprised he could not believe this could possibly be their own. They could not believe that their lives had just changed overnight to an amazing dreamland.

Patrick laughed. "Yes, dad I didn't tell you because you are the king and queen of this palace!" he said as he stopped the car.

They all descended from the car. This was indeed a palace. The house was excessively big and beautiful with twenty-four rooms. It was surrounded by a flower garden with a lawn and a swimming pool at the back. There was also a nice river running through the farm. It was indeed big and beautiful, and the Andersons were proud of their son.

Patrick took them inside the house. He led them to the kitchen where they found the farm workers waiting there for them together with the housekeepers. His parents discovered that Patrick had asked them to so that he can introduce the new Master and Mistress of the farm. He introduced them and afterward they all went to their respective job cheerily. The workers had a feeling they had lovely bosses because they seemed to be knowledgeable about the farm work.

He showed his parents around the house and to their bedroom, the master suite. They found their luggage there.

"But Patrick who brought our bags in?" asked his mother.

"Ohh mum it is that man I said is your butler. That is his job. I am sorry I thought I explained mum." ended

Patrick. His mum could not believe that she who has been someone's servant for as long as she can remember, has people working for her. It felt good and nerve-wracking at the same time. She needed time to get used to this lifestyle.

"Welcome home Master and Mistress Anderson. Unfortunately, I cannot enjoy this stay with you any longer. I have to go back to the city to prepare for work tomorrow. "Patrick was sad to leave his parents and happy at the same time that he has finally given them the gift of which he had always dreamt. He was leaving two happy people. People that matter most in his life.

He left after having a chat with his parents some more and talking about the work in the farm.

"Bye sonny. We will also get down to business tomorrow. Today we have to get used to the new place and the people around us," said his father.

"Bye," said Patrick and left heading for the town.

His father already had ideas of what he wanted to do and how he will make everything work. He was happy that he has helped and he vowed to be a better boss than Mr.

River. His father loved farm work and he was good at agriculture. Patrick was happy that he had settled disputes with his parents and his next mission was to find his wife and apologize whether she takes him back or not.

Chapter 3

When Linda put down the receiver, they both laughed at the way she had responded to Patrick.

"That was excellent of you Li. What gave you that idea?"

"Ohh that was easy Terry. I want him to suffer the way he made you suffer. Let him reap what he sows," replied Linda but a certain thought came to her.

"That is great. How come your face is clouding? What are you thinking about?" asked Teressa.

"It is something that Pat said. He sounded very worried and in great pain. It sounded real. He said he loves you very much and he is asking you to come back home. What if he was serious as he sounded? What if he is genuinely sorry?" Linda sounded worried. They sat in silence thinking.

Then Teressa said "He might have been pretending Li, you cannot be sure. Even if he was serious, I am not prepared to go back yet. He really hurt me, and I do not trust him"

"I hear you. What are your feelings towards him?" asked Linda.

"Truthfully Li, I love him. I have never loved anyone like him. I just cannot bring myself to go back to the kind of life that he gave me." Teressa said with pain in her voice.

"It is all up to you honey. I was not asking you to go back. You see one has to be honest with themselves. As long as you are being honest with yourself you will find a way. Let us have tea while I am waiting for Jim to come and pick me up." They went into the kitchen.

"What are your plans then Terry? Do you wish to go back to work, or you want to relax first?" asked Linda as they drank tea.

"I want..............................," Teressa was cut mid-sentence by the doorbell.

"This might be Jim," said Linda. "Come in!" She shouted.

"What's up Li? Today you call me in without coming to welcome me with a kiss?" complained Jim, Linda's boyfriend. "Ohh Terry!" he said surprised to see Teressa. He had not realized that Linda had company.

"Hey Jim! Glad to see you," Teressa tried to respond cheerfully.

"Glad to see you too. You look so thin what's up? Where's Pat?" Jim could not contain his surprise. He had never seen Teressa looking so thin. He had known her to always be a healthy young woman always full of life. He thought she might not be feeling well.

"Pat is at home," replied Linda. Teressa had become too emotional to speak. She just wanted to cry. It was too painful for her to see other people happy when her life is falling into pieces. Linda told Jim the whole story including the telephone conversation.

"You did the right thing, Linda. Let him suffer the consequences of his actions. Terry, I am sorry to hear this. What are you intending to do then? File for divorce?" Jim was even more surprised about what he heard about Patrick. He could have never imagined Patrick to be that kind of a man. He felt sorry for his girlfriend's sister. That is what Linda and Teressa called themselves. They even told their boyfriends that they are sisters.

With pain in her heart, Teressa said "I do not know. Linda also asked me the same question. I think it is best I look for a job for now and then take time to think about the rest. What do you think about that?"

"I think," paused Jim as he just remembered something "Let me see, the Fashion Essentials manufacturers are looking for a sales executive. Do you think you can do that job?"

"Yes, I can. Remember that was my job before I got married!" Teressa said with a glimmer of excitement and hope in her. At least things would not be as bad if she gets a job in the field that she is passionate about.

"So, what do we do?" asked Linda. She knew that she had to help her friend who had helped her at a time when she was in need. Teressa had paid for her school fees using the money that her mother had left for her. She wanted to return the favor.

"Let me call Steve, the guy who asked me to help find a good person for the post," said Jim as he headed towards the phone. He dialed the phone number.

"Hello!" answered someone at reception.

"Hello, may I talk to Steve please?" asked Jim.

"Hold on," he was transferred to Steve's office.

"Hello," Steve's voice came on the line.

"Hi Steve, good morning. It is Jim." They exchanged some pleasantries. "I just wanted to ask if you have found a candidate for the sales role?"

"No Jim. Unfortunately, I have not. I was deciding on advertising to other newspapers because I am becoming desperate, and it is taking too long. Have you got someone in mind?" asked Steve.

"Hmmm I see. There is someone here that I know. Her name is Teressa Evans. She used to work for the Ludo clothing factory before she resigned when she got married. Do you remember her?"

"Ohh yes. Is she looking for a job?" Steve could not believe his luck. "She was the talk of the industry. I know how good she was. My sales department is in shambles and needs a wake-up call and I know she will be the best to bring us back up if she is available for the job." He continued hoping he was not daydreaming and hoping she will take the job.

"Yeah, I know she is capable. She is seeking a job. When can she see you?" asked Jim with a smile of pleasure.

"Right away!" Steve nearly screamed onto the phone with excitement. I will not even ask for her qualifications. Just tell her to bring copies for my files. Jim thank you ever so much man. You have made my year. I owe you big time!" he could not believe his luck that morning.

"Okay Steve. I will tell her. You're welcome, mate. You owe me a beer!" Jim was happy to be the bearer of good news for both parties.

"Bye" they both hung up pleased with the phone call.

Jim returned to the girls to tell them the good news. The girls saw the beaming smile on his face and knew it was good news before he even said anything.

"What's the news?" Teressa was the first to ask with hope.

"Well let us just say you got the job. Your reputation precedes you and they did not even ask for an interview. They have asked you to bring copies of your qualifications right away. So, get ready and go girl," he said proudly.

The girls cheered and Teressa felt happy. They finished their breakfast and Teressa went to change into a business suit and they all went their separate ways. When she arrived at Fashion Essentials, Steve who was her new boss told her to start work immediately. She appreciated that as it came as a welcome disruption from the pain in her heart.

She kept so busy organizing salespeople and women. Planning what needs to be done and so forth. She checked their books to see how things were done originally and whether there were done properly as the sales team had not had a leader for a while. She updated what she wanted to be done by everyone. She aimed to inspire everyone in the team to be effective salespeople.

When it was time to go home every evening, she would be exhausted to the bone. She was a hard worker determined to do her job thoroughly. Her boss was pleased for trusting his instincts and the rumors he had heard about her. She was also pleased with her own work and did it to the best of her ability. No pain in her heart could take away the passion she had for her job.

One evening she got home, tired. She found Linda was not home yet, so she decided to have a bath and then go and cook a meal for both of them. The housekeeper had already left for the day and the house was noticeably quiet. It was a welcome sanctuary after a busy day at work. As she was about to finish cooking Linda arrived.

"Hi Terry? What is for supper? Smells good in here," Linda called as she was coming in.

"Hi Li. It is fish and spinach." Teressa replied smiling.

"Sounds good because I am starving here. Have you finished cooking?"

"I'm making the final touches to the fish"

Linda did not bother to take her handbag upstairs to her bedroom. She sat down on the kitchen table and waited for food. They did not bother going to the dining room for their meal either.

"Tell you what Terry! Pat called me at work today asking about you. Do you think it is wise to keep him in the dark about your whereabouts?" said Linda.

"Yes, Li we have to. Despite our soft hearts, we cannot tell him. We have to convert our hearts to hard ones." Teressa did not even want to talk about Pat.

"Well, I do not know. I will try. For how long do you want us to keep this up?" Linda asked.

"For as long as we can or until he finds me himself if he is really looking for me in the right places."

"I see. Anyway, how is your new job?" Linda could tell that Teressa was not interested in the subject of Patrick and changed it to a favorite subject. They talked about Teressa's job and Linda's job and many other things. They even had a chant about Linda and Jim's relationship. Later they went to bed.

Patrick kept calling Linda to ask about Teressa. Sometimes he would turn up at the property personally. During those times Teressa will hide in her room knowing that Linda will not allow Patrick to search their house. Her job kept her remarkably busy so much that she forgot about the troubles in her life. After a month at work, she had made some improvements at work and in her health. Her sales team had improved, and their work was starting to show a good improvement. Her bosses were impressed with her.

Linda was starting to see Teressa differently. Teressa was starting to look fatter than when she first came back. She looked round at her midsection. Linda suspected that her friend might be pregnant. She kept her suspicions to herself because she did not want to rock the boat. Teressa seemed really happy and that was important to Linda. The other difference was that she was always sick. Certain foods she did not like their smell and she would throw up occasionally.

"Maybe I'm about to be a godmother." Thought Linda

One day Teressa wanted to wear her old jeans and they felt tight. She tried to force them up, but they would not buckle up. She tried on another pair, and they too were small. She tried another outfit and same results. The floor was piled with clothes. She was surprised because she had not realized any difference in her body, and she had not paid any attention to herself lately. Blaming anything she felt for working too hard. She then started to think hard about other things that have been happening. She thought about being sick and hating the smell of food, especially meat. She had thought she might be turning to a vegetarian.

"Or I might be pregnant!" she thought. *"But that is impossible. It was only once!"* she mussed. She went to check her calendar and discovered that she had missed 3 months of her period. It downed on her that she might truly be pregnant.

The thought of having a baby and the thought of who is responsible filled her with pain. She felt a lump in her throat. She cried and did not know whether the pain was of joy or sadness.

"What am I going to do? Maybe I should ask Li. She might have an idea" thought Teressa. She then chose to wear a flared skirt that hid her bulging belly and a matching blouse. She went downstairs barefoot and planned to spend the day at home as it was her day off.

Linda had prepared lunch for them. Whenever they were off, their housekeeper was given an off day too. Teressa set the table for two. Linda brought food. Linda tried striking up a conversation but Teressa was quite and seemed too preoccupied. That day she felt very withdrawn than the days gone past. It was clear that something was troubling her.

"Terry, what is wrong with you today? You are not yourself," asked a worried Linda.

"Li, I think I'm pregnant" Teressa replied quietly.

"What?!" It was surprising to hear her suspicions said aloud.

"I said I think I'm pregnant,"

"Are you joking? But you are not." Linda asked and answered herself. She had not wanted to believe her suspicions could be true. "When did you find out?"

"Just now when I tried to wear my clothes. Most of them do not fit."

"Wow, how many months?"

"According to my calendar, it is 3 months. "Terry paused "What am I going to do Linda? I do not want to tell Pat!"

"But the baby is his too. You need to tell him," said Linda

"I know but remember he said he is not ready to be a parent. I do not want to be forced to make a decision that accommodates him and his feelings. "Teressa was thinking that she might be asked to have an abortion.

"That was his talking then. According to the way he talks about you now and searches for you, I doubt that he is not ready for it. I think he is. Just give him a chance to know and make a decision too," said Linda.

"No!!" Screamed Teressa. "Sorry I did not mean to shout but I am not going to do that. I will keep this baby and I will manage on my own as a single mum like my mother did. Promise me that you will not tell him no matter how tempted you are?" she pleaded.

"I will not, and I promise to keep my promise to you. But just know that I do not support the idea of single parenting when both parents are alive. I am here and I will help you. I am glad to be a future aunty possibly. Congratulations" Linda said with a smile that did not seem sincere and her congratulations did not sound enthusiastic. But Teressa let it slide.

"She smiled and said "Thank you Li. Tell Jim that you and he are going to be god parents!" she said lightening the mood.

"I will do that. Rules and regulations of pregnancy are that you must keep happy for the baby to stay healthy!" Linda said and they both laughed.

"Well let me do the washing up and take a nap. I feel sleepy," said Terry getting up and gathering their dishes.

"Alright, I am on my way to meet Pat, to look for you. Girl, I am tired of this pretending. It is killing me, and the guy is suffering," said Linda.

"Please do not get tired. It will be over soon" Teressa encouraged.

"Bye," said Linda as she picked up her handbag and walked towards the door.

They held onto their promises.

Patrick kept searching and searching to no avail. He felt like Linda was not helpful at all. He was beginning to give up on ever finding his wife. Teressa and Linda managed to keep him at arms length. It downed on him that she might not want to be found.

After 3 months of searching for his wife to no avail, he gave up. He did not want any women either and some ladies who tried to get his attention did not succeed. He buried himself in his work. He worked hard and he was praised by his bosses and loved by his workmates.

As time went on Teressa was growing bigger and bigger and showing. The baby would play in her womb, and she would smile at the thought that her baby was alive inside her. She and Linda made preparations for the baby. They bought all the necessary things bit by bit. They bought a coat bed, clothes, the lot. At 6 months even a small child could tell that she was pregnant.

One day, when she was at work, one of her sales ladies did not come to work because of chest pains. So, she took over her duties for that day. She took her timetable to see what she needed to do. One of the places she had to go and deliver to was called B and F Hypermarket. Their order was quite big, and she decided to do it last because she knew that if she starts with that one she will be tired and will struggle all day. At least if she does that one last, she will go home straight after.

The list of clients was long, and she planned her calls accordingly so that she can manage them very well. She did as planned, calling a customer briefly before leaving for delivery. She took a thirty minutes lunch in between her visits. She was feeling tired and was going to her final visit.

She arrived at the B and F Hypermarket. Her heart skipped a bit when she thought about it. She wondered why she felt weary of going there.

"I wonder why I don't want to go to this place," she thought to herself. She was feeling tired and needed to rest and the baby was complaining. "Let me finish this and go home," she mused.

Her car was loaded with the stock, and she drove off and went to B and F Hypermarket. When she arrived, she went to the reception and waited to be shown to their buyer's office.

"Excuse me madam," she said to the lady at reception. "Good afternoon."

"Good afternoon, madam. May I help you?" asked the receptionist.

"Yes please. I am here to deliver stock from Fashion Essentials"

"Ohh, I see. Please go to the buyer's office. Go straight on the corridor, when you are two doors to the end of the corridor look to your right and it is the office written seven on the door," directed the receptionist.

"Thank you. Do I just go in or do I have to wait if he or she has a client in?" Teressa asked not sure what was expected of her.

"It is he, ma'am. He has no clients, and he might be preparing to go home. Just knock on his door and he will let you in. I will call him and tell him to expect you."

"Thank you, Miss, or Mrs.....?" asked Teressa

"Mrs. Clevelands ma'am."

"Thank you, Mrs. Clevelands. I am Miss Evans" said Teressa using her maiden name. She has resorted to using her maiden name for fear of Patrick tracing her.

"My pleasure," answered the receptionist. She noticed the discrepancy in the name because she knew Teressa from the newspapers but did not say anything.

Teressa went in the direction she was given. She knocked on office door number 7.

A familiar voice told her to come in. She went in and stood still.

"It can't be Pat!" she thought. She did her best to pull herself together and remember why she was there. She moved forward to greet him and do her duties.

Patrick was dumbfounded. Teressa looked as beautiful as ever. In fact, she looked more beautiful. "She is pregnant! Ooh my how happy I will be if it is mine given the opportunity" mussed Patrick totally in his own world and forgetting all the anger that he had for his wife leaving him the way she did. When Teressa moved forward towards his desk, his heart skipped a bit.

"Good afternoon, sir!" greeted Teressa with the best smile she could master under the circumstances.

"The name is Pat; it has not changed. Good afternoon. How can I help you?" his heart was pounding so hard he thought Teressa could hear it.

"I am from Fashion Essentials. I came to apologize for Miss Lance's absence and for not having the order delivered at the agreed time. She is not feeling well and is not at work today, so I brought the goods instead." She finished breathlessly. "Pat is more handsome than I remember. Ohh how I love the bastard" she thought.

"Ohh, I see. Apology accepted. Thank you." Patrick was not bothered in the least about the sales lady who was absent or bothered about the delivery that came late. He was thanking his lucky stars for making this possible for him to see his wife again at a time when he thought he will never see her.

"Let us see the goods. Are they in your car?" he asked.

"Yes sir" she deliberately used the word sir and ignored the command to use his name. Pat stood up and went round the table, only realizing that he forgot to offer her a seat. He apologized and Teressa brushed aside his apology.

He moved towards the door going past Teressa and making sure he brushes the sand at her side. The small movement sent a load of emotions running through them. He was glad to know he still had strong feelings for her. He motioned her to follow him outside to the parking lot. They went to the car and off loaded the goods. Patrick went to check if they were enough according to the invoice. Patrick called staff to help him off load the goods.

When they finished Teressa said "Here sign this please" giving him the invoice.

"Thank you," he said. He retained a copy and handed the other copy to Teressa.

"It's my pleasure" she accepted the invoice. And bid him farewell and went on to enter her car to leave. When she was about to go, Patrick touched her shoulders and stopped her.

"What is it?" she asked nervously. She did not know whether he will beat her up or what. His touch was sending a thrill of pleasure down her spine. She wanted to remove his hand but could not. She thought about the baby inside her and remembered that this is the father. She almost smiled but had to control herself because she did not trust what he was going to do. He fitted the role of dad perfectly.

"Why did you run away?" he blurted the first thing that came into his mind. It is not the question that he wanted to ask. His eyes were sparkling either with anger or frustration. Even he could not tell how he really felt at that moment.

"None of your business" she replied curtly.

After that retort answer, he went silent for a while. He still held on to her. He was thinking hard. Treating Teressa was easy for him, but he never knew that she too can be as cruel as not telling him about the baby.

"Where do you live? I have been searching for you all over since the day you left and had no hints about your where abouts. Had I known that you work for our supplier I would have come for you right away," Pat could not pretend anymore. He loved the girl and here she was right in front of him. He needed to know where she lives so that they can arrange to meet up and talk about their marriage. He wanted to apologize for everything and was hoping she will forgive him.

Before she could think, she blurted out the answer.

"At my old home with Linda." She was even surprised at herself because she had no intention of telling him anything. She bit her lower lip and wanted to cry after this. She removed his hand with a jerk. She went into her car and Patrick stopped her from closing the door by holding onto it firmly.

"What's the rush?" he asked in the deep sexy voice that she loves so much.

"Pat, just leave me alone!" she wanted to shout but knew that shouting will catch the attention of passersby. Her eyes burned with tears.

"I love you, Terry!" he said quietly. Teressa could not believe her ears. She thought he was going to shout at her. His voice was so sweet, soft, and incredibly quiet. He closed the door with a soft thud and turned and walked towards his office. He wanted the message to sink into Teressa's head. He intended to go to her and Linda's house. He was not going to tell them when he went there so that she cannot hide from him. The intention was to catch them off guard. He was planning to go during supper time because he knew they dined at 7pm and they might not be expecting him.

Teressa remained crying. She looked at him until he disappeared into the building. She let the tears fall down her cheeks unchecked. She did not believe it was Patrick who said those words to her. She loved him too, but she did not tell him. She did not have the opportunity to tell him.

She switched on the ignition and left. She got home and found Linda had already prepared dinner. Teressa did not want to talk to anyone and just greeted Linda and went upstairs to her room. Linda noticed that and did not ask her and left her as she was. To Linda's surprise, Teressa did not come back down for supper. She decided to go upstairs and check on her.

Teressa was sobbing hard. Linda found her like that.

"What's wrong Terry?" Linda asked.

"Li, this is becoming difficult for me. I cannot bear it" she said crying.

Linda was not following. She thought that maybe she meant the baby.

"What's difficult?" she asked.

"Pretending to be away from Pat" Teressa replied wiping tears off her face.

"I told you before that it is going to be difficult. Why now? What happened to make you feel like this now after all these months? You do know that crying is not healthy for the baby. What happened?" Linda asked worriedly.

"I saw him today. He looked as handsome as ever and I almost ran into his arms. Li, am I going mad? She ended with a question.

"No darling. You are not going mad. It is perfectly understandable. Where did you see him?" asked Linda surprised.

"At B and F Hypermarket. One of my sales ladies was not at work today and I did her work. That is how I met him."

"What was he doing there?" Linda asked.

"He works there and is responsible for buying." Said Teressa with a sigh.

"What a surprise. Maybe he was telling the truth before you left. You should have investigated before leaving" said Linda shifting the blame to her friend.

"No Li. That was impossible. Remember I was forbidden from using anything. How was I supposed to do any investigations? Besides, if he was working there, why did he keep it from me?" asked Teressa. She continued, "I love him, Li. Staying here with my belly growing, knowing he is responsible is too much sometimes for me to manage. What am I going to do?" she asked without particularly wanting an answer.

"Well call him and apologize friend. He wants you back remember? He will take you back," said Linda half-hearted.

"With my big belly?" Teressa doubted it. She did not feel as attractive as she was before. She thought Patrick did not want any children, so there was no way he will want her back.

"Yes Terry, with your big belly. I know he loves you and he will look after you very well with your baby. Maybe even better than last time," said Linda.

"The strange thing is that he said he loves me and dashed off without even waiting to hear my response. What does that mean? How can he be shy to tell me he loves me if he meant it? What if he said it to mess with my mind?" All the questions that she was asking herself came tumbling out.

Before Linda could respond, they heard a knock on the back door. That is the door that Jim liked to use.

"It must be Jim. I wonder what he wants at this hour. These days he is acting strange. I know you are hungry, let go down and feed you and that baby." Linda voiced their thoughts. Teressa did not protest. She felt better after talking to Linda. They went into the kitchen where Linda had laid out the food. Teressa then realized how hungry she was. She went straight to the table, sat down, and went on to serve herself while Linda went to open the door for the caller.

"Pat!" exclaimed Linda. She had not expected to see him on their doorstep. Teressa raised her head with a start when she heard that. She too had not expected to see Patrick anytime soon.

"It is me, Linda. Can I come in?" asked Patrick. Linda stepped aside and let him in. Teressa remained seated looking down at her plate.

"Ohh how beautiful she is and to think that this beautiful person is carrying my child," Thought Patrick as he went straight to her and kissed her on the forehead.

"Hi sweetheart," he greeted. Teressa did not respond and kept looking down at her plate. She continued for the sake of the baby even though she did not feel like eating anymore. He pulled a chair and sat down next to her without waiting to be offered a chair.

"Hi Pat" greeted Linda.

"Hi Li, how are you?" he replied.

"I am good thank you. What can we do for you?"

"I came to see my wife" he replied.

The room went silent. It felt like they all wanted to see how Teressa will respond to that. She kept quiet and continued eating. When she finished, she lifted her head and asked, "Who is your wife If I may ask?"

"You Terry, you know that." Said Patrick very patiently.

"As from when?" Teressa had not felt like a wife and did not think that title fits her anymore and Patrick did not deserve her as his wife.

"Is that a question you can ask me? Don't you know an answer to that?" Patrick knew that this meeting was not going to be an easy one. He was prepared to do whatever it took to win her back. He had to play the hard game too and not give up easily. He was determined to put his family back together again. Now that there is a baby on the way too.

"Excuse me guys" Linda interrupted when she felt like her presence was not needed. "Jim asked me to meet him. I will be on my way. See you later." She lied so that she can leave them alone to talk.

"How is he?" asked Patrick.

"He is fine." Replied Linda.

"Okay Li say hi to him." Said Teressa. She knew that Linda was lying and knew her motives. Linda took her bag and left and went to Jim's house. She explained to Jim her reason for visiting without prior arrangement and Jim understood.

Chapter 4

Back home Teressa and Patrick had to settle disputes.

"Terry tell me why you left without my knowledge at least leaving a note to tell me why you left or where you were going?" began Patrick.

"Because I wanted to go," she replied.

"That is not a good reason. Just tell me why please?" insisted Patrick in an extremely low voice that terrified Teressa. She thought he might beat her.

"Well, if you have to know because I was afraid of you. You beat me up every day and I was so tired of your abuse. Did you expect me to live that way for the rest of my life?" Teressa responded with so much pain in her heart. She decided it was best to speak her mind and get it over with. There was no point in keeping it all inside when she needed him to know what his actions did to her.

Patrick's eyes changed from anger to a deep emotion of regret. When he looked at Teressa, emotions ran through his body. It was the same feelings he had the first time he met Teressa.

"There was no need for you to be afraid of me Terry," he said. "I love you and you know that. Don't you?" he asked.

"No, I do not. How can you beat someone you claim to love? I have every right to be afraid of you. How can you lock me in a house like a prisoner in a place that is meant to be my home of peace and happiness? How long was I supposed to be patient? What was I being patient for anyway? Six months of hell Patrick, you subjected me to. No!" Teressa was getting angry the more she thought about the treatment she received at the hands of this man in front of her.

"I'm sorry Teressa" Patrick apologized. He now realized the extent of his actions.

"Do you expect me to believe that?" she shouted. The guy did not seem sincere.

"Listen Terry. I....................." she cut him off.

"Listen Teressa! What do I have to listen to? Listen to your telltale? Listen to you lying to me? And you expect me to believe your lies? I am tired, Patrick. Just leave me alone," she finished breathlessly. She was sobbing.

Patrick went to her side and brought her into his arms. Teressa tried to protest to no avail. Patrick waited for her to calm down before speaking.

"Please let me explain Terry" he begged her. She nodded in acceptance because she did not trust her voice.

"It was like this Terry................" he told her about his upbringing and his escape from home and how he joined the gang. He spoke about his life journey and how he felt when he met and married her. When she heard all this, she felt so sorry for the little boy who did not have it easy in life. She felt the pain deep in her heart. She felt the pain as if it was her own experience. She listened quietly without interruption so that he can tell it all. When Patrick paused, she said.

"Why didn't you tell me in the first place?"

"I am sorry Terry, I thought you were going to leave me. I was afraid of losing you. I wanted to quit the gang and get a job then I would tell you everything after." Pat felt a surge of hope when he saw her relax.

"This is sad Pat. I would have understood," she paused. "What happened next?"

He told her of his fear when she saw the letter, of why he became hostile towards her as a defense mechanism. He told her of the day he quit the gang and that it was the day she left the house. He explained the pain he felt and how he was feeling when he kept looking for her and not finding her.

He told her about getting a decent job and how he was happy and wished to share that joy with her. He told her how he went to apologize to his parents and the farm he bought for them.

"So, when I saw you today, I could not believe my eyes. I was so overjoyed. You are still the most beautiful woman I have ever seen. Why did you and Li lie to me? I have suffered so much needing you in my life so that I can apologize to you and hope you can forgive me. My wish is to live a beautiful life with you." He ended.

"I wanted you to suffer the same way I suffered when I was living with you. I also did not want you to find me because I did not trust you. I thought you do not love me," she said. This time her voice was soft. It was the voice that Patrick missed so much. She now understood his suffering and felt the need to hold him closer in her loving arms. She wanted to soothe him as if it were only just happening. She wanted to murmur loving words telling him that it was all over and he must not worry anymore. Instead, she just remained where she was.

"I hear you darling. I do not blame you for that. I did not think, and fear clouded my judgment. I am so sorry!" Patrick said with pain in his heart.

Teressa could not hold it back any longer. She went to him and held him in her arms. Patrick responded positively. They remained like that for a long time without speaking. Patrick brought his head down and kissed her. She opened her mouth willingly. It tasted as good as they both remembered. Even more than that. It made her believe in him all over again. She fell in love all over again. Patrick raised his head. He sat down and put Teressa on his lap.

"But Terry this is not over yet. Even you never told me about your past when we first met and during our marriage. Now is a suitable time for you to tell me as well please," asked Patrick. He wanted to know her better. He felt that as he had told her everything, he needed to know everything about her too if they were to get over their differences. He did not want any more secrets between them again.

"I am sorry Pat, that was bad of me. I never spoke about my past because I never thought about it," started Teressa. She was the kind of person who never spoke about herself unless prompted. She believed in listening to the other person and never thought her life story was worth talking about.

"I was brought up by a single parent. But my story is not as sad as yours," she continued.

"That is okay. Continue" prompted Patrick.

"My father died before I was born. My mum brought me up on her own. She worked for a clothing factory in New Zealand. So, she was not struggling or that poor. My dad had left her a villa. Her parents had also left her some property. After dad died, mum sold the villa," she said.

"How did your father die? Did he know he and your mum were expecting a child?" Patrick interrupted.

"It looks like he knew in the letter that he wrote to my mum before he died. He had asked mum to keep their baby safe until they meet again. My mum said before she received the letter, she did not know that she was pregnant. So, when she received the letter, she checked her calendar and was surprised that she had indeed missed her periods and it was funny that my dad knew." She paused and they both smiled at that sweet tale.

Teressa continued "My dad was a soldier and he died in the war"

"I'm sorry," said Patrick

"No need to be. I never knew him except in photos. It is sad that I never got to know him, but he made sure I was cared for so that made it better for mum and myself. So, after mum sold the villa, she lived in the house in town and that is where I was born and brought up. It was quite a big house with lots of rooms about twenty rooms and three helpers. So, it was good."

"Sounds like it was a pleasant childhood," said Patrick.

"No," she said. "It was boring. I was not even allowed to make my own tea or coffee. I was bored a lot. Too much space but with no one to play with. At the age of seven, my mum got me a private tutor. So, I was home-schooled. He taught me 5 days a week and then at the age of eleven I was sent to a boarding school. That made it better because then I was around other children and learned to socialize." She took a breather, and she was thirsty.

Teressa stood up and went to pour herself a drink. She offered another one to Patrick who politely declined.

She continued "When I was at school, doing form four, I was called from home and told my mum was seriously ill and she needed me to come home. Linda was my best friend. She was an orphan and had lost both parents to a car accident. So, she accompanied me home so that I am not alone in my time of need. Unfortunately, my mum died a day after I arrived home. She had had a heart attack and could not survive it. I was left alone in this world." Teressa felt sad remembering those terrible moments that she lived.

"Mum left everything to me but it was not enough because I wanted my mother back," She continued.

"Where were your relatives?" asked Patrick. He was wondering how such a young girl cannot have anyone to look after her from the family circle.

"They were all in France. They came for the funeral and left. They could not take me because I did not have a passport and I guess they had their lives to live. They just left instructions with our helpers to contact them should I need them."

"That is a shame," said Patrick. He could not believe they would have done that. He thought some families have no care for one another.

Teressa continued "After the funeral, I went back to school and completed my O'levels. I continued at the boarding school to do my A'levels. Linda had social welfare payments for her fees when we were doing O'levels. But they were not going to continue when she went to do A'levels. So, she asked me to help her. And I paid for both our fees, and we continued with our education. I sold our house because I felt like it was too big for me on my own without my mother."

I went on to do salesmanship in college and University and Linda studied Law. I rented a flat here in town in Switzerland and we lived together. Mum had left me a fortune which I was able to use to pay for our living and our fees, for both Linda and me. We decided to buy a house together and Linda offered to pay for the house herself to return the favor, but I would not take it because it would not feel like my place too. So, we met halfway. That is how we ended with this house," she ended her long story.

Patrick looked at Teressa and thought of a sixteen-year-old left to look after herself with no one in the world. He felt sorry for her. He had listened attentively all along playing with Teressa's silky absent-minded. He kissed her on the lips for a long time. When he stopped, he said,

"Well sweetheart, that is sad and the good thing is that you had some money to help you along the way" he paused and seemed to be thinking hard. His mannerism changed and he became serious. He said, "Terry there is one serious thing that you did that I am not happy about."

"What have I done now Pat?" Teressa was surprised at the sudden change of mood. She got scared.

"Why didn't you tell me about the baby, our baby?" he asked sounding a bit angry.

Teressa got angry too. He had no right to ask her that. "Whose baby? How was I supposed to tell you? Do you remember what you said that night?" she waited for him to respond and when he did not, she continued.

"I will tell you. You said you are not prepared to be a parent. So do not worry your pretty head. This is my baby, and I will keep it and bring it up on my own."

"I am sorry Terry. It is not because I did not want to have children. It is because I did not want to have children as a robber parent. My children would have been called children of a bastard. Their lives would have been in danger constantly. I just cannot bear that," he took a deep breath. A sign of his anger abating.

"I want this baby as much as you do," he was realizing how deep his actions had been. He felt bad that this would have cost him the love of a beautiful woman and the ability to watch his kid grow. He sounded sincere like he meant what he was saying.

"Okay darling. I love you, Patrick. I cannot stay away from you any longer. This was killing me. I wanted to call you and tell you, but I was so afraid. I longed to see you and just to see your face. I thank God for making us meet today. It might have been coincidentally, but I will treasure it." Teressa said in a light mood.

"Ohh Terry, I love you more than you will ever know. I apologize for everything I did to you. Thank you for the patience you had with me. Thank you for keeping my baby. That means the world to me. I am so happy that I am a future dad." Patrick said happily. The anger and pain were all forgotten.

They spoke about a lot of things for a long time. The tension between them was growing.

"Pat let's go and sit in the lounge, my back is tired," said Teressa.

She switched the television on, and they sat down on the carpet and put cushions around them.

Patrick could not keep his hands off her any longer. He pulled her towards him. He kissed her deeply. His hand found its way up to her breasts. She was not wearing a bra. He cupped the breasts. He moved his lips up and down her spine. He sucked her nipples one by one. They caressed for a long time. They undressed each other.

Patrick played with her under parts. She felt weak with need. She tickled his manhood. Patrick felt like bursting with a hunger for her. At last, he entered her fully. He started moving about inside her. She was fully engrossed with emotion. Her body itched with emotion. They made passionate love. Afterward they lay spent in each other's arms panting. They were both satisfied. It was really the lovemaking of two people deeply in love.

When their breath was even, Pat said,

"Sweetheart, may you please come home with me? I cannot live without you anymore." He was pleading with a sweet voice. That was one thing that Teressa loved about him. He had a beautiful voice that could melt even an icy heart. It made her smile even if she were hungry.

She smiled and said, "Yes darling." She agreed with an equally sweet voice. She just knew that she could not stay away from him any longer either.

"I have to inform Linda. But before I make any concrete agreement, promise me one thing?" she asked him.

"What? Anything," he asked.

"Promise me that you won't ask me to leave my job and that we will get house help to help us at home?" she asked.

"Yes darling, I promise. It is up to you what changes you want to make in our home. I will rely on you as you know best. I really care about you and your happiness. I promise to do everything in my power to make you happy." Patrick knew that he was going to work hard to make up for the terrible times he had subjected her to.

They promised each other to give themselves a good life together. They promised to talk about things and not to keep secrets from each other. Then they went upstairs to sleep. They spend the next day together planning their future about the baby and planning baby names. It felt good. It felt right.

Chapter 5

Linda returned a day later on a Sunday. She found Patrick there and knew instantly that things might have been worked out between her best friend and her husband. She envied them. She could not bear any children and as a result she envied Teressa and Patrick for having a baby on the way. Her boyfriend had been talking about children a lot lately and she knew that could be the beginning of the end of the relationship with a man that she loved.

Linda came in as Patrick and Teressa were making breakfast. They exchanged pleasantries and Linda joined them for breakfast. Patrick decided to tell her about their getting back together and going home so that they can leave early.

"By the way Li, Terry and I are leaving today," he began.

"Why? Is everything okay with the two of you so quick?" she sounded surprised. It felt like she had wished that they separate forever.

"What is the surprise, Li? I told you that I love Patrick," replied Teressa. "I cannot stay away from him anymore. Remember I am even carrying his baby and it makes sense that we bring it up together" Teressa did not like the way Linda responded to the news. She had expected her friend to be happy for her.

"I know Terry. I am sorry. It is just that after all you told me, I did not expect you to go back to him. I suppose you know best" she tried to sound light but inside she was not pleased at all.

"Good luck and Congratulations on your baby Pat," she tried to sound a bit cheerful but did not succeed. Teressa took at as maybe the thought of living on her own again.

"Thank you, friend," said Teressa going to give her friend a hug which was half-heartedly received.

After breakfast, Patrick and Teressa packed her belongings and the baby's stuff. When they arrived at their home, it was to be happy as the first day of their marriage. They found a maid to help out in the house. Teressa kept her job. They lived happily to their promises. The time came for Teressa to give birth. She took 3 months maternity leave from work. They were blessed with a baby girl. They became the happiest couple ever. They named their baby Lisa. Linda pretended to be pleased to be baby Lisa's godmother. Her relationship with Jim had ended because Jim could not see a future together without children in it. So deep down in her heart she was not happy for her friend. Envy and jealousy seemed to rule and control her.

Lisa was a healthy baby, bustling with energy. Her parents were happy to have had her. She was a perfect likeness to her grandfather, Patrick's father. Patrick's parents were over the moon for having a grandchild and they dotted on her and their daughter-in-law.

Teressa loved her in-laws greatly. They were like dear parents to her. She loved being around her inlaws as it gave her the love she never had as a child of having both parents loving her. She felt like Patrick's parents were a blessing to her. She visited them most of the time. This made Patrick the happiest man ever when seeing his family happy together.

One day Teressa decided to visit her friend on a weekend when they were both not working. She took the baby with her, but Patrick did not go with them.

"I am glad to see you, Terry. At least today I get to have company. It is boring being on my own all the time. Especially weekends when I do not even get to go to work." Said Linda when Teressa and the baby arrived at her home.

"I was missing you my darling friend. Since you and Jim split, we have not had a good catch up. I am sorry about that my dear. Life is so busy with a baby," said Teressa cheerfully but sad for her friend.

"That is not a problem. There is no need for you to be sad for me because you are leaving a happy life," that stunk, and Terry wondered what Linda meant by that.

"I am not talking about me Li. I really mean it. I know how difficult it is to be ditched by someone that you really love. What is the need to be cut with me?" Teressa had to ask.

"I am not cut, Terry. I am sorry if I sounded that way. Hi Lisa...." said Linda changing the subject and shifting her attention to the baby.

They spend the entire day together. During the evening, Teressa went back to her and Patrick's home with their baby Lisa. The day had turned out to be one of the weirdest days she had ever spent with Linda. She had never felt so out of place ever when she ever visited Linda. It took her by surprise. And for the first time in her life, she felt afraid of Linda. Linda had acted strangely all day long, saying nasty remarks and she kept on referring to Teressa's life as being a good life.

"I wonder what makes me feel like this. Linda has been my friend from school, but I have never seen her like this. Today she was different," she thought. *"Maybe it is because of Jim. She might be missing him terribly."* She mussed as she drove home.

When she arrived home, she told Patrick.

"Maybe you need to be careful around her darling. I always knew she is jealous of you. Not sure if she is dangerous but just be extra careful when you are around her," said Patrick. He had picked on the animosity or nasty comments that Linda always said when Teressa talks about something. But he too had not taken it seriously because his wife did not seem to notice, and he did not see any harm there. But now he was weary that Teressa notice today and realized it must have been bad.

"I hear you, darling. I will try by all means," she replied.

At midnight Teressa woke up with a start. It was as if she was hearing someone screaming. It was indeed the baby screaming. In that instant, Patrick also woke up with a jerk.

"What is it, Terry?" he asked startled.

"I do not know Pat; it sounds like the baby is in pain. This is not her normal cry!" she said worriedly.

"We need to go check on her Terry, not just talking lying down!" shouted Patrick and Teressa jumped.

She ran to the baby's cot bed. When she looked at the baby she stood still. The baby's face had turned blue, and the eyes were sunken deep into their sockets. She shuddered. When they went to bed the baby was as healthy as ever. This sudden change surprised her. When she thought of her baby dying her heart skipped a bit and she fainted.

Patrick jumped out of bed and ran towards the baby's cot bed where the baby was crying, and Teressa was slumped onto the floor. His heart was beating so fast as he ran faster than a bullet. He wondered what was happening. He could not understand why the crying of their baby could make his wife faint. It was just too much.

When he got there, he saw what Teressa had seen. He wanted to faint himself. He started crying. He had to be brave and act fast if he were to save his wife and his baby. He ran to the phone and called the ambulance and the doctor. While waiting for the ambulance he ran back to the bedroom, and moved his wife into a comfortable position on the bed. He went on to pick up his baby. It felt like he was touching a burning fire. The baby's temperature was too high. He could not hold the baby for long in his bare arms.

His skin felt like it was being cooked. He then took a blanket to use to hold baby Lisa. He tried to comfort her. But the baby was in too much pain to be comforted. Her cry was shrill. She cried and cried until the ambulance and the doctor arrived.

The doctor got scared upon examination. He had never seen such an illness. He sent the baby straight to the hospital. He then attended to Teressa. She came round and looked around surprised to see the doctor there. His mind was lost in what was happening. When she started to recall she jumped and set upright.

"My baby!" she cried.

"Okay, now little one. Drink this first Lisa is in safe hands on her way to the hospital," the doctor replied while giving her some water to drink.

"But I have to be with her," Teressa protested.

"No, my darling," this time Patrick replied. "You will go but first concentrate on your health, okay?"

"No Pat! Lisa needs me. She is ill and I have to be with her," she protested still.

"Relax, Mrs. Anderson. The baby will be okay. You will leave as soon as I am sure you are fine. Now rest for a bit while I follow the baby to the hospital" said the doctor pacing his things in his briefcase. "I will call you as soon as possible. Now Mr. Anderson, see to it that Mrs. Anderson rests please," ordered the doctor as he ran to his car.

Teressa could not rest. Her mind was on the baby. Patrick tried to soothe her. Deep down in his heart, he knew that the chances of the baby surviving were slim from the state in which the baby was. If there was it was very slim.

The doctor drove like a mad man to the hospital. He knew that the baby's illness was unnatural. He had never seen anything like that all his carer life.

"*The baby might be poisoned,*" he thought to himself.

When he arrived at the hospital it was too late. The baby did not even make it to the hospital amid all efforts to keep her alive. Unfortunately, she died. The doctor's thoughts went back to Teressa. He wondered what will happen to her when she hears the news.

"May I see the baby please?" the doctor asked one of the nurses.

"Ohh yes doctor, we put her in Forester in ward B. We thought you would want to examine her because this death seems unnatural, and we are afraid the body will go bad fast," said the nurse.

"What do you mean go bad? The baby just died?" asked the doctor" doctor was surprised.

"Like I said doctor, the death is unnatural so please go quick," begged the nurse.

The doctor did not ask anymore. He went straight to where the baby was putting on his gloves and mask. What the doctor saw was strange. The baby already had an odor coming out of it. He ordered an immediate post-mortem.

The baby was moved to the pathologist's office and a post-mortem was performed. When the doctor received the results, it confirmed his suspicions. The baby was indeed poisoned.

The thought of informing the Andersons about the death of their child was too much. He knew they were going to be broken. He had to do it though before they come to the hospital. He had no choice but to call them as soon as possible.

"Hello" Patrick answered the phone.

"Hello, Mr. Anderson, this is Doc"

"Ohh yes, doctor. How's Lisa? Is she going to be okay? We were just about to come over as my wife feels better now." Patrick wanted to know that the baby was fine.

"I'm sorry Mr. Anderson," is all that the doctor could say. He heard a deep sigh at the end.

"Say it, doctor. Out with it!" prompted Patrick. He wanted to hear it in words as he sensed the doctor's hesitation.

"I'm sorry Patrick, the baby didn't make it," finally the doctor said it.

It was as Patrick had expected. But hearing it said aloud hurt a lot. He loved his baby so much. It felt like his heart was being pulled out of its strings. How was he going to tell his wife? He just kept holding the phone.

"Pat are you there?" the doctor forgot about using last names. He knew that at a time like this, people preferred familiarity.

"Yes, doc I am here. What happened? What killed her?" his voice was so low, distant, and sad.

"I am deeply sorry Mr. Anderson. She died on her way to the hospital. Lisa was poisoned," said the doctor with sadness in his voice.

"What? She was what?" Patrick almost screamed at the phone.

"The child was poisoned, Mr. Anderson. The police must be informed so that they investigate and get to the root of where the poison came from."

"I see doc. I will do as you say. How about the post-mortem? Will it be able to show what kind of poison is it?" asked Patrick. He was seething with anger. His voice was shaking with pain and unshed tears.

"It has already been done. The results will be told in due course. All I can say is that the child was poisoned." Ended the doctor with an apologetic voice.

"Why so early doc?" Patrick was surprised.

"Well, the body was rotting so fast. The poison is very deadly. Not anything we have seen in this country. We are going to check what it is, then reports all of it at once," said the doctor.

"Thank you for everything doc," said Patrick. He needed to get off the phone and go to his wife.

"It is fine Pat. Take care of Mrs. Anderson. I will see her tomorrow."

"Okay. Thanks again doc." He replaced the receiver. The baby was poisoned and rotting within a few minutes! It was too much for Pat. How could he tell Terry? This was heavy for him. He had lost his beloved child. He would not want to lose his beloved wife when she hears the news. He stood there for a while pondering how he will deliver the news to his wife.

"Pat, what is wrong? Are you still on the phone?" Teressa called. Surprised that Patrick was taking too long to return.

"I'm coming sweetheart," he replied in a shaky voice. He started pacing up and down. He could not bring himself to face his wife with the sad news. There was nothing he could do though. He had to tell her eventually. The longer he delayed the more nervous he became. He had to do it now. With that, he went to the bedroom to Teressa.

"Well, Paṭ who was it?" Teressa asked with much difficulty. She sensed the answer in the tension that was in the room.

"I'm sorry Terry!" he paused. It was the longest painful pause. It was difficult to break the news. Teressa was already shaken by the baby's sudden illness.

"What is it, Pat? Is she dead?" she asked in a voice full of pain.

"I am sorry Terry. Doctors could not help her. Lisa did not even make it to the hospital"

Pat could not even finish the last sentence.

"Ohhh! My child Pat!!! I want my ch...............!" She could not even finish her sentence. She was sobbing so hard. Patrick tried soothing her to no avail. He was hurting himself. They had lost their only child. Something has killed their baby.

All they knew was that it was poison. They could not even think of where the poison came from. They tried to figure out what the baby ate and through pain and anger, they could not think straight.

Lisa's funeral arrangements were made, and she was buried a week later. Patrick's parents, their family members, and friends attended the funeral including Linda who was supportive of her friend. She seemed distraught about losing her goddaughter. The funeral was a memorable day for

Teressa and Patrick. It was the last day they set their eyes on their only child. It was a pain that no one could heal.

Patrick's parents stayed for 2 days after the funeral to help the couple before returning to their farm. Linda stayed with them for a little while longer. Teressa lost the beautiful smile that she always wore. Patrick lost his humor. There was no longer any joy of Lisa's laughs and cries in their life anymore. The house was airily quiet.

Chapter 6

The telephone rang and Pat rushed to pick it up.

"Hello!"

"Hello, Mr. Anderson. This is doc" replied the person on the other side of the call.

"Hello doc! How can I help you?" asked Patrick surprised that the doctor phoned them.

"Ohh yes, Mr. Anderson. As I said before, baby Lisa's death was unnatural, so the matter was reported to the police who have started an investigation." He paused.

"They have done their bit at the hospital, and they will be coming to your house tomorrow. So, I just wanted to inform you to look out for them." said the doctor.

"Thank you, doc," replied Patrick. "I am glad they will look into this. My daughter deserves justice."

They both hung up. Patrick went back to his wife. He informed her about what the doctor said, and they waited for the police to come.

"I think it's time for me to return home," Linda informed them in the afternoon. "I hope my being with you guys has helped, but it is time I return home and back to work." She ended.

Teressa sighed. She knew that life goes on. She loved having her friend with her. It helped her not feel so much pain and Linda had been so good in consoling her since the death.

"That is fine my friend. Thank you so much for being there for us and putting your own life on hold. I really appreciate you," said Teressa hugging her friend. Patrick also said his goodbye. It felt sad that they are now just the two of them with no baby and none to distract them from missing her.

Later in the evening, the police came to ask them questions about what happened to baby Lisa. They told them as much as they could remember about the day and what happened the days before.

"The day before the death, "paused Patrick remembering, "Terry and baby went to visit our family friend and Lisa's godmother. Linda was not nice to them all day"

"What was different about that day" asked detective Brown.

"We usually visit her, and we have fun, and we chat and play with the baby and all. But this time she just seemed a bit offish," replied Teressa.

"What do you mean offish Mrs. Anderson?"

"She was a bit nasty with her comments. She would say unkind things. But I understand because she had just broken up with her boyfriend and so maybe she was just unsociable. It is nothing really," said Teressa.

Patrick added "This does not mean that she would poison our baby. She loves her to bits. She is her godmother" they did not want to believe that their best friend could be responsible for the death of their child. It was impossible.

The police spoke to them a little bit longer and took Linda's address and left.

"Do you think Linda could have done this?" Teressa asked her husband.

"No. She might not be nice sometimes, but she is definitely not a killer" Patrick replied to his wife. "She could not have. She loves you like a sister and you have been there for her most of your lives. No way she could hurt you like this. She has no reason anyway." He was trying to convince his wife as well as himself.

Weeks went by and the police could not find the source of the poison. They questioned Linda and could not find any motive to kill the baby or any trace evidence that she ever had any poison in her possession.

Even Patrick and Teressa were also interrogated as suspects, and were also eliminated. The hope of ever knowing what happened to their baby faded. There was no establishing where the poison came from.

The case went cold. Life went on. Patrick went back to work and Teressa too eventually went back to work. Life at home was no longer the same. The joy that was in their home was gone. They were just existing. Their love for each other held them together. They stood by each other and saw each other through the pain.

After a few months, Teressa did not feel well and decided not to go to work. Patrick was worried because his wife was not someone who misses work.

She was throwing up and felt weak and dizzy all the time. When this went on for more than 3 days Patrick suggested that they see the doctor. He was worried that maybe the poison that killed their baby has found its way into Teressa's system.

"Congratulations Mr. and Mrs. Anderson. You are expecting a young Anderson" the doctor was smiling when he told them the news.

Patrick and Teressa looked at each other. They could not believe it. A baby is on the way. They had not even thought of trying for another baby. They were still mourning their lost baby. They could not think about how it even happened. All this time they were just surviving seeing no future. Happiness washed over them.

They thanked the doctor and went home. The drive home was quiet. Neither knew whether to be happy or sad. They did not know whether they wanted a baby or not. It felt surreal to them.

When they got home Teressa wanted to sleep. She felt physically and emotionally tired.

She said, "what have we done Pat?"

"Nothing sweetheart. We have been blessed." Replied Patrick. It had started to sink in that he is going to be a father again. Teressa had not looked at it that way. All she thought about was what she has done. All she could see was the death of her baby and could not see why she gets to be given another chance to be a parent.

"What if this baby meets the same fate, Pat? What if we are not meant to be parents? What if.................?"

"Do not say that. We are meant to be parents. That is why we have another chance. What happened to baby Lisa is a tragedy and no fault of ours," said Patrick not liking the way his wife was thinking.

"But we let her die!" It was the first time Teressa spoke aloud about her guilt of losing her baby. Somehow, she thought it was her fault. She thought she should have protected her child from whatever it is that poisoned her. She panicked thinking that she might lose this other baby as well.

They spoke about it some more with Patrick and vowed that no matter what they will protect this baby by all means. When they got used to the idea of being parents again, excitement kicked in. They wanted to share with the world.

They phoned Patrick's parents, and they too were so excited that they will be grandparents again. Teressa then decided to tell her best friend. After all, she was her only family.

"Hey Linda, it has been a while. How are you?" asked Teressa when Linda answered her call.

"Hey darling. It has been a while indeed. How are you?" Linda did not sound as enthusiastic as Teressa was to hear her voice.

"I am good Li. I have some news to tell you!" Said Teressa with excitement in her voice.

"Do tell friend, I can't wait to hear what you have to say," Linda replied.

"I'm going to be a mother again!" Teressa was practically screaming the words down the phone.

The phone went silent on the other side. Teressa thought maybe Linda was not feeling well and she had to ask her if she heard what she said.

"I have heard you, friend. I am happy for you." Linda replied in a dry voice.

"You do not sound happy. Are you okay friend?" asked Teressa.

"Yes Terry, I am fine. I am just worried. We lost another baby and you have got yourself pregnant again. What if we lose this one too after being happy," Linda spat the words down the line. She was fuming.

Teressa could sense Linda's anger. She thought her friend could be angry because of the loss they had. She never thought it was anything deep. Teressa understood as well because she had the same thoughts when she first found out that she was pregnant.

She replied "I understand friend your frustration. I felt the same way too when I found out I was pregnant. I did not plan for this. It just happened. Once you get used to the idea, please be happy for me. I need your support friend." Teressa wanted to convince her friend, but she thought it better to give her time to get used to the idea.

Linda changed the subject and they spoke for a little while longer.

"At least let me look after you friend. You know I care and love you." Said Linda.

"Of course friend, I will. You know Pat is here too. It will be like old times. But this time we have Pat right from the beginning so it should be a better experience." Teressa replied. Not understanding what her friend was getting at about taking care of her when she lives with Patrick and not having any complications with her pregnancy.

They hung up and both went on to do their own things. A month went by when they had not seen each other. They would speak on the phone. Teressa's bump was growing smoothly. She had no complications and had even started preparing for the baby. The excitement of having a small person at home running around was growing with each passing day.

Linda was increasingly becoming distant from Teressa. Teressa was getting worried about that. She was, however, too busy with her life to even notice that her friend was distant.

One weekend both Patrick and Teressa were bored, and they decided to visit Linda. Linda agreed that they should get to her. They planned to spend the whole weekend and properly catch-up. When they got there Linda was happy to see them and seemed more fussy than usual. Teressa thought that it could be because she was pregnant, and her friend had come to accept that.

They watched a movie and Linda went to cook for them. Teressa followed her to the kitchen so that she can help prepare food as she always does.

"Ohh no Terry, stay here I will be as quick as I possibly can. You need to rest and look after our little one. I will do the cooking. It will be a simple quick meal" Linda convinced her.

Teressa went back to the lounge and watched a film with Patrick. Linda brought food and served each one of them. They ate while chatting at laughing. Everything seemed good.

After eating Patrick offered to take the dishes to the kitchen and he washed them while Teressa and Linda stayed in the lounge. Patrick felt a little off and he did not think much of it. He went back to join the two women when he finished doing the dishes.

They started playing a card game and Patrick felt a little sweaty. He then asked if the two ladies felt okay.

"Are you guys okay I feel a little hot" he said.

"We are fine, Pat. Is everything okay?" Asked Teressa.

"No. I think we need to go home. I am sorry Li we will not be spending the weekend anymore." He said to Linda.

Teressa became worried about him. Linda tried to convince them to stay. Patrick refused. He was thinking about what the doctor said and what the police suspected about someone close to the baby having poisoned the baby. He was worried that he might meet the same fate. He needed to take himself to the hospital straight away.

"If it helps Linda give us the food you cooked, and we will eat that tomorrow because we are not planning to cook tomorrow as we had not made plans to be home." He said to make Linda feel better about them leaving so soon.

Linda seemed to like that idea. She quickly went into the kitchen and packed two lunch boxes and labelled them.

"Well Tell, as you can see, these are labelled. So, I do not want you eating Patricks food because you need a special diet for our baby," said Linda.

That seemed odd. Patrick already had his suspicions but kept them to himself. He looked at his wife and she did not seem to notice anything.

They said their goodbyes.

"Bye my darlings. Even though I am not happy to see you go. I thought we were going to spend our weekend together because I missed, I missed you a lot." Said Linda.

"I know Li, we love you too. We will be back soon. Or you come to us soon." Said Teressa promising that they will come together again soon.

"I know you will! Said Linda smiling.

They left. Patrick asked Teressa to drive because he seemed to be getting worse with each minute passing by.

He said to Teressa "can you please take me to the hospital darling. I think I have been poisoned"

"What?!" said Teressa. She nearly crashed the car when Patrick said that. She had not noticed anything amiss. She just thought it was odd that Patrick said he was not well and asked to go home instead of going to sleep in Teressa's bedroom that is at Linda's house.

"What do you mean you think you have been poisoned?" she asked touching his forehead. He was burning up and sweating.

She turned the car and rushed to the hospital. At the same time calling the police. All she was thinking about was that she will not lose her husband, the love of her life. Not like her baby. Patrick spoke to the police as they were going to the hospital.

They called the detective who was investigating the death of their baby and he promised that he will meet them at the hospital.

By the time they reached the hospital, Patrick was out of breath and getting worse and worse. Teressa was crying and feeling hopeless. Detective Brown and the hospital staff were waiting at the entrance with a wheelchair to take Patrick into hospital in. They were worried that if Patrick had ingested the same poison as his daughter, he might not make it.

Patrick was rushed into the emergency room followed by Teressa running after him. The doctor wanted to drain the poison and try to save Patrick's life before too much poison goes into his blood. They did and by the time, they had drained every drop off food that in Patrick's stomach, Patrick was in so much pain that he had to be put into an induced comma.

In the meantime, detective Brown was talking to Teressa trying to figure out what had happened and how they might have suspected that Patrick was poisoned. Teressa told him everything she could remember.

"You say Linda made the food herself and none of you ate from the same plate? Asked Detective Brown.

"Yes. Ohh which reminds me, she gave us food to take home and she put it in different lunch boxes, and I thought that could be odd because it is the same food. But what seemed odd is that she made sure that she asks me not to eat Patricks food" said Teressa when she remembered the food that Linda had given them.

"Where is the food now?"

"It is in the car. We drove straight to the hospital because Patrick suspected that he had been poisoned and needed to get here as soon as possible." Teressa replied.

"You did very well. It is good that Patrick noticed that. I am glad you called me as well because now we can narrow down the possibility of where the poison is coming from with it being in such a narrow window." Finished Detective Brown.

"Mrs. Anderson?" called the doctor from outside the emergency room.

Teressa got up from the waiting room and went to the doctor.

"Is everything okay doc? Is my husband?" Teressa was dreading to ask. She felt sick just thinking of what the doctor could say. She did not want to hear the words she heard when they lost their baby. She did not even want to think about losing Patrick.

"I'm sorry, it is not good news" started the doctor. Teressa wanted to faint. She had to gather all her courage to keep listening to the doctor. She stirred at the doctor and could not even bring herself to ask any questions.

"It's not what you think" continued the doctor realizing that Teressa might be thinking of the worst case. He saw her give a sigh of relief. He continued "We have had to put your husband under induced comma so that we can try to flash the remainder of the poison out of his system without having it putting a lot of strain on his organs." He paused. "We do not know what damage has already been done to his organs. We just know that we have drained every article of food from his stomach and what is left is what had already entered his blood stream. Like I said before, this poison is deadly. Your husband was lucky because he is older and had not ingested much of it and he had noticed really early," ended the doctor.

Teressa looked at him for a while trying to digest what the doctor had just said.

She was jolted back to the present by the detective asking the doctor a question.

"So, doc, you are saying the poison that Mr. Anderson took is the same as that killed the baby?"

"I suspect so. I will not be able to say for sure until tests have been done. But I suspect so," the doctor said. "We will send the samples of the drained contents to the lab for testing.

"There is food that Linda gave us. Is there a way we can have that tested too?" asked Teressa when she could find her voice. Her mouth felt dry. She was shaking thinking of what could happen and refusing to think her friend could do this to her.

"I will take these to our lab for testing Mrs. Anderson," said the detective. "We will share the finding with the doctor. I will appreciate it if you do not tell Linda because we do not want to spook her. If she is guilty, she might try to run. Let us keep her in the dark for now," asked detective Brown.

Teressa agreed because she was already thinking about that too. She then motioned for them to go to the car so that she can give them the food with the different labels. Teressa then went back to the hospital waiting room to wait for her husband to get better. The hospital staff tried to ask her to go home, and rest and she could not bring herself to going back home. She slept on a chair next to Patrick.

Chapter 7

The next day she woke with a stiff neck. The nurses convinced her to go home and change and get some food. They mentioned that she needs to look after herself for the sake of the baby.

Teressa agreed after they had promised that they will call her as soon as Patrick woke up. When she got home, it felt quiet and airily. She ran a bath and sat in it letting hot water burn her skin. She cried and cried because it all felt too surreal. She was worried that she might lose her husband. She was worried about losing her friend if it turned out that she poisoned her husband and her friend. At the same time, she wanted her to pay if she did.

Linda was like the only family she had besides Patrick and his family. She had so many questions that she would like to ask Linda but knew that she could not ask her. After a while she came out of the bath because the water had gone cooler. She went to get dressed so that she can go back to the hospital.

She heard a knock. Her thought was to ignore the knock. Then she thought it could be the detective. Her heartbeat so fast because she thought something might have happen to Patrick. She panicked and ran to the door. It was Linda.

"Friend" is all she could say. She did not know what to do or say. Let her in? confront her? Scream at her and shake her until she says what she has done? She knew though that she could not do that without jeopardizing the case. She tried to compose herself.

"Sorry to come unannounced friend." Said Linda while they were still at the door. "I was worried about Patrick and thought I should come and check on you guys," she said.

"Ohh come on in," said Teressa trying her hardest to get herself composed.

"Where is Patrick? How is he?" asked Linda.

"He is at work" is all that Teressa could think of saying.

"Ohh, I thought he was not well, and it is a Sunday?" Linda asked suspecting that her friend is not being truthful.

Teressa did not want Linda to know where Patrick was as agreed with the detective. She said "He was not well last night and seemed better this morning. But there was an emergency at work, and they asked him to come in and sort it." Linda was looking at her funny.

"At least that is what the note he left me said. I was asleep when he left" said Teressa trying to say something that her friend was going to believe.

"Okay friend. Let us hope he is not cheating on you because he will have me to deal with" said Linda trying to make light of the situation.

"And me" they both laughed. It took all Teressa's energy to even smile at Linda. She wanted to strangle her and felt guilty for feeling like that because she had no evidence that her friend had indeed poisoned her daughter and her husband.

"Ohh my word, where are my manners? Come on in" said Teressa when she realized that they were still at the doorstep.

Linda laughed and said, "I thought I was no longer allowed to come here!" jokingly.

"I am sorry friend. I do not know where my brain has gone. It must be this little one taking all my intelligence away from me." Says Teressa.

They went in and Teressa offered to make them breakfast.

"Well, you said you did not want to cook today so we can have that food that I gave you last night. After all, it is past breakfast time," said Linda.

Teressa realized that it was nearly noon.

"Sorry friend Patrick took the food with him because he needed it seeing that he will have such a long day at work." Teressa thought fast of a response to that request. "Let us go for brunch at the coffee shop just down the road. They make lovely coffee and this little one loves their sandwiches like crazy" Teressa added patting her belly.

Linda agreed and they took their bags and left. At the coffee shop, they chatted a bit and Teressa kept checking her watch. She wanted to be in the hospital and not where she was. She texted detective Brown about her situation and asked him to contact her if there was any update. Linda noticed that Teressa was distracted, and she thought that it could be because Patrick was at work on a Sunday.

"If you look at that watch one more time it will speak to you." Said Linda jokingly, when Teressa did not hear what she had said and glanced at her watch instead.

"I am sorry friend. I am a bit distracted, and I feel a little bit tired. I think I will go home and have a lie-down. Do you mind if we spent some time together another time?" Teressa could not pretend anymore to be enjoying herself when she was not. She wanted to go.

Linda agreed and they walked back to Teressa's house. Linda took her car and went back home. Teressa went to the hospital when she was sure that Linda had arrived home. It was good news when she arrived at the hospital.

Patrick was alive and awake. They had woken him up a few minutes earlier. She ran to his side and hugged him.

"Ohh Pat, I am so glad you are here with me. I was so worried about you. How are you feeling?" sobbed Teressa.

"I am getting there my darling. Thank you for rushing to the hospital and for believing in me when I asked you to" said Patrick in a hoarse voice.

"Why wouldn't I believe you?" asked Teressa.

"Linda is your friend, and I was worried that you might think I am accusing her of something she is not" he replied.

"Remember we were suspicious of her for losing our baby. How can I not believe you? Are you sure you are okay?" Asked Teressa worried about Patrick's voice.

"I am okay. My voice is like this because of the tubes that they had put down my throat." Replied Patrick.

They heard the doctor clearing his voice from the foot of the bed. They both turned to look at him.

"Mr. Anderson you are very lucky." He began. "The poison had not hit your vital organs yet. We managed to drain all of it from the food that was in your stomach. There are still some traces in your blood stream. But it is no longer dangerous to you. You will however have to take it easy in the next few weeks, drink a lot of water and these pills that I will give you to wash all of it from your body. We will have to monitor you so that we can see how much damage was done to your stomach or any other vital organs."

"Thank you, doctor. Should we expect a full recovery though?" asked Teressa.

"Yes, we expect a full recovery. I would suggest being careful what you eat at the moment because we do not want you to eat that again; I cannot promise that your organs will be able to handle another one. No matter how small." The doctor said.

"Thank you, doctor. I will try my best to look after myself. Does this mean I can go home?" asked Patrick. He did not like hospitals and did not want to be there more than necessary.

"Yes. I will ask the nurse to complete your discharge document. But you will have to come for a review every week as an outpatient until I am satisfied that you are okay."

"Thank you, doctor. Have they found out if it is the same poison?" Teressa asked wanting to be sure that Patrick going home does not mean that they will stop checking the poison.

The doctor "Not yet Mrs. Anderson. But I assure you. The minute I get the results I will let you and the detective know." The doctor concluded and excused himself after giving instructions to the nurse to discharge Patrick.

They went home after being discharged. Teressa told Patrick about Linda turning up at their house. Patrick was worried that she might have planted the poison in more of their food.

"I did not let her anywhere near my kitchen Pat. I took her to the coffee shop at the corner of our house," Teressa assured him. They had to divulge a plan of how they will keep her away from them until they are sure it is not her that was poisoning them.

"What if I have a genetic mutation that reacts to certain food and then it turns out to be poisonous to my body?" Asked Patrick trying to come up with other possible alternatives for why he and his baby got poisoned in the first place.

Teressa understood where he was coming from. She had also tried to think of any alternatives, but she could not find any. "We do not know that Pat. Let us not make any assumptions or come to any conclusions until we get the results of the tests. Let us just keep ourselves safe and not eat any new food or anyone's food," Teressa said.

"We will stay away from people. Especially Linda. I will take time off work and you should too. Anyway, the doctor said you should take it easy. You have no choice but to take it easy." Added Teressa.

"I understand Terry. That is all we can do." Agreed Patrick.

Days went by without them hearing from the hospital or the police. They were getting worried and wondering whether they should call the police or the hospital and ask. They had managed to find ways to stay away from Linda. Teressa told her that Patrick was fine but not home. When Linda offered to spend time with her, she told her that she just wanted that time to sleep as she is tired a lot and does not mind Patrick not being at home. That seemed to work.

The doorbell rang one day when they were chilling in the lounge. It was detective Brown. Patrick asked him to come in.

"You look much better Mr. Anderson. How are you feeling?" asked detective Brown. When he sat down on an offered chair.

"I am feeling much better thank you for asking." Replied Patrick. I feel like the poison is out of my system now." He continued. "How can we help you?"

"I have come to tell you of the results of the tests that we did." Detective Brown paused, took a deep breath, and continued "it seems the poison you ingested is the same poison that killed your daughter. I need to ask you both some questions."

"I'm not surprised," said Teressa.

"What do you mean?" asked detective Brown.

"The symptoms were similar although they were mild on Patrick." She spoke.

"Is there anything similar to what you did at the time when we think your baby ingested the poison and to when your husband ingested it too?" Asked detective Brown.

"We were at Linda's house both times. Linda offered to cook for us both times. Linda served us both times. It is a no-brainer!!" Teressa said with tears in her eye. Tears of anger that her friend could have done this to her. Anger at herself for Letting it happen for the second time if she did. Anger at herself if her friend had not done it and it was all a coincidence and she just suspected her friend for nothing.

"I understand your anger and frustration, Mrs. Anderson. But I have to say at this stage, everyone who was present is a suspect and that includes you. You and Linda did not ingest the poison. At this moment in time, I need to ask you questions about how?"

"You are saying my wife poisoned our baby that she loved so much and then poisoned me?" Patrick was angry at the detective. He loved his wife and was confident that she loved him enough to want to spend the rest of her life with him. There was no way she could have poisoned him. "Did you test the food that Linda gave us?" he asked.

"I understand your anger, Mr. Andersson. At this moment in time, we cannot rule anyone out. We need to get all the facts. We tested the food and there were traces of poison in both lunch boxes. But it was not enough to have any effect on anyone unless they already had the poison in their system. Also if ingested in the amount we found, after a while it would have eventually killed the person." Detective Brown explained patiently.

"It's okay Pat. I will answer any questions they ask of me. I know I did not do anything wrong. So, I should not fear being asked any questions." Said Teressa. "What about Linda, when are you going to ask her?" she asked.

"Thank you, Mrs. Anderson. You will have to come to the station with us. My colleagues have gone to take Miss Linda to the station, and I was informed just before I came here that she is now at the station waiting for me." Replied detective Brown.

"I'm glad," said terry. Thinking that Linda could have run off.

"Mrs. Anderson, I have to take you to the station with me as well, please. You are not under arrest. You are coming with me to be asked questions so that you can be eliminated as a suspect. We all suspect who the culprit is but with her being your friend, I must be sure that you did not do this together and eliminate you," said detective Anderson.

"I cannot believe you will say this to my wife," said Patrick not liking the thought of his wife poisoning him.

"You will be surprised Mr. Anderson how many cases of poisoning we get whereby a partner is the instigator. Like I said, we need to eliminate your wife from the suspect list. I am sure you both appreciate that we leave no stones unturned to get you justice"

Teressa was not worried and did not mind going with them. "Of course, I will come with you. I want my baby's killer to be put behind bars" she said in a voice full of passion.

After those words, there were no more arguments. They left and went to the police station. Patrick followed in his car. When they arrived at the station, Teressa was put in the interrogation room separate from the one where Linda was. Patrick was not allowed in the interrogation. He was in the adjoining room where he could listen to the interviews.

Teressa was asked if she wanted a lawyer and she declined. She knew she had nothing to hide. Detective Brown asked her the same questions as to what he had asked her before. About what had happened prior to Patrick being poisoned. He asked her about their reason for visiting Linda. Teressa explained their relationship with Linda and that there was no reason they could not visit her as she was practically her sister. They owned the house that Linda lived in together.

Detective Brown was listening with his colleagues and Patrick was watching with another one of the police officers. The purpose of asking Teressa was to also watch her body language. At the police station, they were police who were trained to tell if someone was lying. They needed them to monitor and give their verdict. Detective Morgan, who was with Patrick, was watching closely and silently.

"Thank you, Mrs. Anderson, for being very cooperative with us. I am going to talk to my other colleagues. I am coming back" said detective Brown leaving Teressa on her own. They wanted to see if her body language will change if she was left on her own.

He and his colleague went to the next room to ask Detective Morgan what he thought.

"I think she is telling you the truth." Said detective Morgan. "Her body language does not portray someone who is guilty. You can see the pain when she is talking about the events."

"I told you there is no way my wife would kill our baby and poison me!" shouted Patrick. He was frustrated with the police for putting his wife through this after everything that they have been through. "My wife is pregnant for goodness's sake. You want us to lose this baby as well?" he asked angrily.

"We apologize Mr. Anderson for putting your wife through this. However, we must do our job. You are free to go to her" said detective Brown. "Now this leaves Linda. If she did this, she did this of her own accord. The question is why?" he said to his colleagues.

"I guess we have to go and question her to get those answers" answered detective Morgan.

When Patrick entered the room where Teressa was, she went straight to his arms and sobbed.

"I'm sorry Pat" she cried.

"What are you sorry for?" asked Patrick confused.

"I brought a killer into our lives!" Teressa replied. She was not thinking that if Linda is the killer, she was equally guilty because she brought her into her life.

Patrick was quick to reassure her "No you did not. Remember we do not know if she did this darling. She could be innocent. Let us not jump to conclusions."

"But Pat, all evidence is pointing to her. What if she did? What am I going to ...."

"Hush darling. Please do not think like that. Think about our baby. I do not want you to be upset" Patrick did not let her finish the sentence because he too did not want to know what they will do should their suspicions be true.

The detectives were watching and feeling sorry for the couple. Their jobs had to be done. When they saw the love between the two, they needed to solve this for them. They needed to give them closure and keep them safe.

They let them go home. Teressa argued saying she wanted to see Linda's interview and the detective said she could not. Linda had not said anything and was refusing to cooperate. Teressa and Patrick went home disappointed. Detective Brown told them that they still had time to keep interrogating Linda before they could let her go if they have no evidence to link her to the crime.

Chapter 8

Linda sat in interrogation silently. She appeared to be composed. As an investigator herself, she knew that her every movement will be monitored. When she went to Teressa's house and did not find Patrick there, she was worried that it will come to this. No one had told her what she was at the police station for. The police officer and woman who had come to her had said there was a problem with her friend, and they needed her help. She had reluctantly agreed to go with them.

She tried to ask them if her friend was fine and they refused to answer. She tried to call her friend and there was no reply. She suspected that this could be it. She waited patiently. She had played this scenario in her head so many times and she knew what she will say.

Detective Brown entered with Detective Morgan. Linda looked at the mand and did not bother to smile.

"Why am I here? I have been sitting here for a long time. For someone who is supposed to be helping, you are wasting my time that I can use for something else in my life. Is my friend, okay?" asked Linda angrily.

"We apologize Miss Linda to keep you waiting. We needed to make sure your friend is okay," said detective Brown. Linda shifted uncomfortably. She thought that maybe Teressa had eaten the food.

"Let's get on with it then," she said to the two men.

"Okay. Let us get on with it then" replied Detective Brown. "As you know that your friend's daughter Lisa died of poisoning, and there has been a new development that we are hoping you could help us with some findings. Before we go there, I just want to let you know that if you do not want to talk to us, you have to say so and we will stop this interview. You can request a lawyer anytime. Anything you say can and will be used in the court of law should the need arise." He needed to make sure that she is aware of her rights because they did not want to interview to go to waste when they cannot use it.

Detective Brown was aware that Linda is a private investigator so she will know the law as well, but they needed to mention that anyway as part of the procedure. "Do you understand?" He asked

"Yes," answered Linda.

"Would you like us to continue?" he asked again.

"What is this about? Am I under arrest?" Linda asked.

"No, Miss Linda. You are not under arrest. At this point in time, you are assisting us with the information we need to help us solve a case of poisoning." Replied Detective Brown.

"I thought that case was closed?" said Linda trying to pry information from the police before she could agree or disagree.

"As I have said Miss Linda there are new developments. That case was not closed. It had just gone cold. Would you like to continue?" asked Detective Morgan.

All this time Detective Morgan was sitting there silently, and he was looking at Linda's reactions. He could sense some uneasiness. He saw through the delaying tactics that Linda was trying to do. As skilled as Linda was in the defense side of the law, the police were skilled to tell when one is being deceptive, is uncomfortable, or is trying to stall an investigation.

Linda looked at him with disgust. She was not liking the man that was in front of her and was trying to figure out a way of getting out of this situation.

"I do not need a lawyer. I am a lawyer myself," she said quietly.

"We know you are a lawyer Miss Linda, but we would suggest you get advice from someone else, not yourself," said Detective Brown.

"I said let us get on with this. I do not need a lawyer." Said Linda. She had decided what she was going to do and did not want to keep stalling. She thought that it was time the truth came out.

"Okay then. We would like you to sign a disclaimer, to say you refused to get a lawyer." Linda signed the disclaimer.

"Now tell me what this is all about," she asked.

"Well Miss Linda, as you know that your friend's daughter was poisoned, it has come to our attention that she was poisoned straight from coming to your house. Mr. Anderson has met with similar circumstances. He has also been poisoned after being to your house. Would you like to explain to us, how that happened to be?" Asked Detective Brown.

Instead of answering Linda asked a question. "Is Patrick, okay? I have not seen them since they left my house?"

"Yes, he is fine." Replied Detective Brown. Linda shifted in her seat.

"Looks like you are disappointed miss Linda?" asked Detective Morgan.

Linda looked at him, looked at Detective Brown, shrugged her shoulders and said, "I was just asking."

"Are you going to answer my question?" asked Detective Brown.

"No," Linda said simply.

"Why?" he asked.

"Because I have no answer to your question." Linda was asking herself how she is going to handle this situation. She wanted to talk but at the same time, she wanted to talk to her friend first.

"Miss Linda, we need to know what happened. You are not helping yourself if you are not talking to us."

"How so?" She asked Detective Brown.

"Because if you tell us what happened, it could make this process easier for you, and we will not be wasting your time any longer than necessary as you said we have wasted your time." Replied Detective Brown.

Linda looked down at her hands and kept quiet for a long time until Detective Brown prompted her to speak. She still kept quiet. They both tried to get her to speak and did not seem to be getting anywhere.

"Well Miss Linda, you said you do not want a lawyer. Do you want us to get you one now?" asked Detective Morgan. Linda kept quiet.

"Would you like us to get you tea or something to eat? We have been here for over six hours, and I am starving," said Detective Brown. Linda just nodded. She looked like someone who had a heavy load on her shoulders. The two police officers left the room.

"Phew, this is one difficult person. I thought she was going to tell us something when she refused a lawyer."

Said Detective Brown once they were outside out of earshot of the room.

"I know. She has something she wants to say. I could tell from her body language. I think she just does not know how to start." Replied Detective Morgan. He continued "We just need to find a way to convince her to let it out."

"We do. I wonder what will happen if we bring her friend in," said Detective Brown.

"I think at this moment, it is not a good idea for Mrs. Anderson because she might get overwhelmed. She seemed too angry, and it could make Linda not talk even more." Replied Detective Morgan.

Detective Brown thought about it for a moment. And said "You are right. Maybe we should just ask her if she would like to talk to her instead."

"Yes. That is a better idea. We could ask her how she thinks her friend will feel if she thought she killed her daughter and tried to kill her husband." They agreed to use that line of questioning and see if that will be helpful.

They got coffees and went back into the room. They brought coffee and a sandwich for Linda. Linda thanked them. She ate in silence, and they watched her.

"Miss Linda, tell me something. Do you think about your friend?" asked Detective Brown.

"What do you mean?" asked Linda. She was tired by then.

"I mean, with you being here, what do you think your friend will say when she hears that?"

"You didn't tell her?" Linda asked.

"No. We did not tell her because we do not know what we will be telling her until you tell us what you want us to tell her. We have to go to her with answers," said Detective Morgan.

Linda thought of her friend and how she will take the news. She thought maybe she was out to talk to her before she tells the police anything. At the same time, she was worried about the pregnancy and how strong or fragile her friend was. She had conflicting emotions. She sat in silence and finished her sandwich and coffee. She looked at both men who also sat with her patiently. She knew that deep down they were not patient. They were just playing a waiting game. Linda also knew that there was no turning back.

She looked at them, let out a big sigh, and said, "I think I am ready to talk."

Detective Brown smiled and said "Thank you, Miss Linda. Tell us what happened" He prepared a recorder to capture the conversation.

"Okay. I will start with baby Lisa." Said Linda. Both men nodded in encouragement. "Teressa came to visit me with her, and I saw an opportunity that I had been waiting for." She paused. "I offered to cook for them. I made a lovely meal because I wanted Lisa to enjoy her last. I put poison in her food. I made sure that I fed her as well so that there was no chance of Teressa tasting the food."

She paused for a long time. "Go on" prompted Detective Brown.

Linda had tears in her eyes. The two men were surprised that she is just confessing to murder, and she is crying. They thought that maybe she is regretting it.

"I put enough poison to make sure that she does not survive. When Teressa told me that she died I was sad because I had lost my goddaughter. And at the same time, I was happy that I had achieved what I wanted to achieve."

"Where did you get the poison from?" asked Detective Brown.

"I learned of this plant from the internet that was poisonous, and it happened to grow by the stream that is not far from our house," Linda said.

"Okay. So how did you get it into your house?" he asked.

"When Teressa told me that they were coming, I went to pick up the plant and kept it in the house to use it when they come." Replied Linda.

"So, you planned to give it to both Mrs. Anderson and the baby?" Asked Detective Brown.

Linda replied "No. I wanted to give it to the baby. I do not want anything to happen to Teressa, I love her."

"But why the baby?" asked Detective Morgan.

"She was the best option," Linda replied. Although both men were not satisfied with the response, they needed to finish with the confession before they ask about the motive.

"Then after a while, Teressa told me she was pregnant again; I was so angry. I was planning what I will do to the baby, but then it downed on me that the babies were not the problem. If I get rid of this one too, she will make another baby with Patrick. So, I had to get rid of Patrick." The detectives could not believe what they were hearing. They had to keep a straight face as professionals.

Linda continued "When they told me they were coming to see me, I did not have enough time to get enough poison that will kill him instantly just like it did the baby because I was so busy. I just rushed to the lake and grabbed the closest I could get so that before they reached my house, I was not in the house. I did not realize that it was not enough to do the damage that I was looking for."

"How about the one that was in the lunch boxes that you gave them?" asked Detective Brown.

That was not enough. I used the spoon I had used to mix Patrick's food to serve that food that I put in lunch boxes." Linda replied.

"Ohh, I see, so you didn't mean to poison your friend as well, because both lunch boxes had traces?" asked Detective Morgan not believing Linda.

"No. Like I said, I do not want anything happening to Terry. I realized I had used the same spoon I had used earlier when they had left. I was not planning to put poison in the food they were taking home because I knew that my friend was going to eat that food." She replied.

"How come you asked your friend not to eat her husband's food that you had labeled his name to?" asked Detective Morgan.

"I always say that all the time when I give them food," Linda said.

"Your friend said this time you were insistent. How come?" he asked.

Linda thought about it for a while and said "To be honest, I did not see it being different. Maybe I was worried that if he ate the food and spat in it Terry might get poisoned too." They looked at her and nodded that they were listening.

"Go on." Encouraged Detective Brown.

"Okay! Then Patrick said he was not feeling well and decided that they were leaving," she said.

"How did you feel about that?" asked Detective Brown.

"I was disappointed because I had planned to go to the stream at night to get more of the poison so that when I make breakfast, I complete what I started." She looked at them to see if they were listening. She continued "when Patrick started complaining of not feeling well, I thought maybe the poison was enough. When they left, I planned to follow them to their house the next day to see if my poison worked." She paused.

"I got to their house and Teressa told me that Patrick had gone to work. I thought that my poison did not do the work. That is all that happened." She concluded.

"Let me get this straight. You say you poisoned baby Lisa, and you poisoned Patrick? asked Detective Brown. Linda nodded.

"Please speak up Miss Linda," he said.

"Yes, I poisoned them both," she replied.

"What were you planning to do, when you heard that Patrick was fine?" he asked.

"I thought my friend was lying to me because she refused to tell me anything about him. I thought she was lying when she said he was fine because she refused to visit me with him or to let me visit them. Probably I was going to try my luck again," she replied.

"When did you find out that he was indeed fine? Asked Detective Morgan.

"Today when you told me," Linda said.

"Now we would like to ask you why you poisoned them. There must be a reason?" asked Detective Morgan.

"I would tell you, but I want to tell my friend. I do not want her to hate me. Maybe if I tell her, she will understand my motives," Linda said. Pleading with the police to let her talk to her friend.

"Miss Linda, you do realize that what you have done to your friend, she might never want to talk to you?" asked Detective Brown.

"If you want me to tell you my reason, you will make her talk to me," said Linda. She knew that she is going to prison. She did not care about that as long as her friend understood her reasons.

The Detectives realized that there is nothing they could do to make her talk to them.

"Okay, Miss Linda. Thank you for being honest with us. Based on your confession, we have to arrest you for the murder of baby Lisa and attempted murder of Mr. Patrick Anderson.........................." Detective Brown said to Linda. He read her, her Miranda rights.

"We will take your request to Mrs. Anderson and let you know what she says."

The Detectives left the room.

"Wow, that is some friend. I wonder what her reason is. Do you think it could have been jealousy?" detective Brown asked his colleague.

"It is usually jealousy. But hers is strange because she is sparing the friend. Maybe she wants her friend all to herself." Replied Detective Morgan.

"Such a shame. I feel sorry for Mrs. Anderson. How will she feel when this information is confirmed?" he sighed. "Anyway, I will go to her house and inform them of the confession and the request.

"Okay! I will go and complete the report and send it to the prosecutors so that court proceedings can begin. I am glad we have finally got to the bottom of this case and justice will be done," said Detective Morgan.

They went their separate ways. Detective Brown went to the Anderson's home. When he arrived there, they were expecting him. He had called them in advance to find out if they were home.

"Would you like coffee Mr. Brown?" asked Teressa. She was nervous. She wanted to know the truth and at the same time, she did not want to know. She did not want to be disappointed.

Detective Brown noticed her fear. He refused the coffee offer and wanted to get it out of the way and leave them to go home and rest. He was tired. It had been a long day.

"What happened detective?" Asked Patrick.

"Miss Linda has confessed to the murder of baby Lisa and an attempted murder of you Mr. Anderson," replied Detective Brown.

Teressa cried. She felt her heart breaking to pieces. She had hoped that the Detective would have said they found a killer, but it was not her friend. As much as she suspected that it was her friend, she was not sure how hurt she was going to feel.

"Why but why?" she kept asking.

Patrick tried to console her. He was hurt too. He too had hoped the news would be different. He had to ask the question that he and his wife had been asking themselves.

"Why? What was her reason for doing this?" he looked at the Detective holding his wife.

"She refused to tell us her reasons and said she wants to tell Mrs. Anderson herself." Replied Detective Brown.

"She must be mad and drunk from her poison. I will never let her anywhere near my wife," said Patrick getting angrier.

"I understand your anger and fear Mr. Anderson. From our interrogation, Miss Linda will never hurt your wife. If you want closure, I suggest that Mrs. Anderson talk to her. But it's your decision. We can leave it to the prosecutors to try and get that information from her in court if you do not feel comfortable meeting her," said Detective Brown.

"There is no way we will see her," said Patrick.

Teressa said "I will never get close to that woman. I cannot believe, she was my friend. After everything that I have done for her. Why but why?" she cried some more. She was hurting so much and could not see herself going to see Linda. "I will see her in court." She concluded.

Detective Brown had done what he had come to do. He left the two consoling one another. Teressa was in so much pain that she could not sleep. Patrick was worried that if his wife keeps on crying, she might lose their baby. He called the doctor who reassured him that, she needs to let the pain out. She has a good pregnancy. She just needs to avoid stressful situations.

Patrick spoke to his wife about it. She knew that but she could not help the pain she was feeling. She did not know whether hearing Linda's reasons will help her feel better. She did not know whether she wanted to go through the trial either. Listening to the details in front of so many people. Conflicting emotions were playing in her mind.

Chapter 9

Linda kept waiting and hopeful that Teressa will change her mind and see her. Detective Brown had informed her that the Andersons were refusing to see her. She understood why they would not want to see her. She was hoping to make her friend feel better. She believed that she was the only one who can make her friend feel better.

As the days went by, Teressa was getting increasingly confused about wanting to see Linda. She wanted to know why she would do such a painful thing to her. She just did not want to see her. Linda was refusing to tell someone who will tell her. She kept insisting on telling her directly.

Teressa was hurt by the fact that they had a home together. She was more than a friend to her. She was her sister. She was asking herself what she will do about their home. Since her friend was in jail, the house was empty, and bills needed paying. Teressa would not even bring herself to go to the house. She would not allow Patrick to go either. She knew that Linda was in jail and would not hurt him, but another part of her heart told her that the house is associated with her pain and could hurt him.

Linda was refused bail. The judge said that she is a danger and did not trust that she will not go to Teressa's house to finish off what she started with Patrick. Linda tried to make a deal and it was refused. A court date was set for her trial to be tried in front of a jury. She got herself a good lawyer. She was not wanting to be let free. She was hoping for a lenient sentence.

Linda knew that what she had done was wrong. She had not planned to be caught. She had planned to achieve her goal and keep on living happily ever after. Unfortunately, it did not happen, and she had to face the consequences. She was just disappointed that her friend was not coming to see her.

Linda asked her lawyer to make a deal with the prosecution. She did not want to go to court. She just wanted to be sentenced without a trial. She felt like a trial was just going to be a waste of her time. The prosecution could not agree because she did not want to tell them why she did what she did. That knowledge was going to help the judge in giving her an appropriate sentence.

Detective Brown kept informing the Andersons about what was happening with the case. Teressa knew that at some point she will have to see Linda to talk about the bills of the house. This meant that they would have to talk about the case. She thought that Linda will mention that. She was also worried about seeing her friend behind bars.

She knew that Linda belonged behind bars but that did not stop her from worrying. She had loved her friend for a long time. She loved her husband and their late daughter as well. She felt stuck in a wheel wind. She was crying all the time. Patrick was increasingly getting worried about her. He thought that they needed to talk to someone close to Linda who might have had an insight into Linda's mind.

"Hello!" answered Jim when Patrick called.

"Hello Jim," replied Patrick. "This is Pat. How are you?" they exchange pleasantries.

"To what do I owe the pleasure of receiving your call today Pat?" asked Jim. He was wondering why Patrick called him because they had never spoken since he separated with their friend Linda.

Patrick got straight to the point of his call. "Did you hear that Linda is in prison?" he asked.

"No, I did not hear. What happened?" asked Jim surprised.

"Well, she……." Patrick told him everything about the poison and the death of the baby and how she tried to poison him. Jim knew of the baby's death, but he did not suspect that Linda was capable of this.

"I am sorry to hear this man. I would have never imagined Linda doing such a thing," said Jim.

"She did and we were all surprised. Now she is refusing to tell the police why and wants to tell Terry herself. My worry is that Terry is hurting and seeing Linda will make her pain worse. I am worried about what might happen to her and the baby,"replied Pat.

"Baby," asked Jim. "Do you guys have another baby?" he asked.

"We are expecting another baby. I am worried that if Teressa keeps stressing, she might lose the baby to a miscarriage. I cannot seem to console her. I am out of ideas. I thought I should ask you who has had a close relationship with Linda, do you think she might hurt Terry?" Patrick asked.

Jim was taken aback. He thought about how much Linda loved Teressa. "No. I do not think she will hurt Teressa. She used to tell me how much she loves Teressa and how much she will do anything to protect her and keep that friendship. She used to tell me that she is where she is because Terry took care of her"

"If that is the case, why would she take something that Teressa loves away from her?" asked Pat puzzled.

"You will have to ask her that. I am wondering that too. She could have been jealous. I would suggest that Teressa must see her. That way you guys will get closure." Paused Jim. "You can accompany her if that will make you feel better," he suggested.

Patrick thought that was the best idea. He thanked Jim and went to tell his wife about the conversation. They agreed that this could be a good idea for them to confront her together. Teressa felt scared of her friend. She felt like she did not know her friend. They called Detective Brown and told him that they want to see Linda and their condition was to go together.

Detective Brown went to tell Linda.

"Mrs. Anderson has agreed to come and see you with her husband," he said.

"No way. I want to see her alone," Said Linda. She did not want to see Patrick.

"Miss Linda, you are going to have to meet her halfway. It has taken a long time for her to agree to see you in the first place," Detective Brown tried to reason with Linda. "After all, you caused her this pain. You cannot expect her to do it your way. At least she has agreed to see you," he spoke.

Linda thought about it. She saw the reason and decided to agree. Detective Brown went to tell the Andersons. A day was agreed upon.

"This way," said Detective Brown when Teressa and Patrick arrived in jail to see Linda. He took them to a room where Linda was sitting at the far end of the room. They sat opposite but were not allowed to touch.

Linda smiled when she saw her friend.

"It is so good to see you, Terry!" she said. Teressa looked at her with contempt.

"*How can she even think it is good to see her?*" Teressa thought to herself. She could not even smile. Instead, she felt like strangling her friend. She wanted to scream at her until she could scream no more.

Instead, she said, "Just tell me why Linda?"

"I can see you are not happy to see me," said Linda. She looked at Teressa and did not look at Patrick at all. "I'm sorry friend!"

"Just tell me why," Teressa hissed under her breath.

Linda knew there was no chit-chatting with Teressa. She looked her squarely in the eyes. "I love you, Terry," she started. Teressa looked at her and frowned. She wondered what games Linda was playing.

"I am not playing games and I know you are wondering why now. I will tell you. I want you to understand where

159

I am coming from. I need you to promise me that you will never hate me," she pleaded.

"I do not promise you anything. How can you do this to me? You are supposed to be my friend and look out for me. We are supposed to look out for each other. How could you?" Teressa was practically screaming at this point. She was getting annoyed that Linda had the audacity to ask her not to hate her. How could she not after everything she had done?

"Please Terry, promise me!" Linda pleaded.

Teressa just looked at her. Patrick spoke for the first time and said, "Just tell us why?" Patrick was worried and had called his parents and asked them to be there for Teressa. He did not know what else he could do. He had hoped that when they leave the police station they will have arrived and will know how to help Teressa heal from all this.

Linda did not even look at him. She addressed Teressa only.

"Terry, I love you like a sister. You are more than just a friend. You are my everything." She began. Teressa looked at her and said nothing. "When you first married Patrick, I was happy for you and thought you were going to stay in my life. But when you did not keep in touch, I was so mad at you. I had Jim then and it made me feel better. When you came back home, I was over the moon. I had you back into my life.

"I hoped and prayed that you stayed with me forever this time. When you were expecting Lisa, I saw you and I raising our little baby together. But when you went back to Patrick, my heart broke into pieces," she paused.

"Linda you were my friend, not my boyfriend!" Teressa could not believe what she was hearing.

"I know. I could not help what I was feeling. You were my only family, and I did not want to lose you," said Linda.

"You knew how much I love Patrick. How would you expect me not to go back to him?" Teressa asked.

"I was only hoping." She continued. This time Teressa could only stare in disbelief. Patrick could not believe his ears either. "When you went back to live with him, I was hoping you will include me in your daily life. But you did not. I lost Jim. I felt like I lost everything. You, the baby, and everything. I needed to find ways to bring you back. Every time we spoke it was about Lisa this Lisa that. I felt left out. I started to hate Lisa for keeping you away from me. So, I decided to get rid of her. Poison was going to be the best way for me. I was hoping it was going to be quick and she would not have to suffer much. Even though she had to go, I still loved her. I felt the loss too. I hurt too like you. But at least it brought us together" Linda was practically crying at this point. Teressa looked at her in disbelief. She and Patrick were at a loss for words.

They could not think. They could not talk. They just stared at Linda.

Linda continued "when we lived together after Lisa's death, those were the best days of my life. I could take care of you. It felt like for the first time in my life I was needed. I could give back from what you gave me all our lives since we met."

Teressa let out a hissing sound "Some way of showing gratitude."

"I'm sorry Terry," said Linda. "I thought it was enough to pay for everything you have done for me. When I had to leave your home, I felt the loss again."

"But Linda you were just a phone call away. Why couldn't you talk to me about how you felt before you thought of killing my daughter?" Teressa still could not understand what Linda was saying.

"How could I tell you that Terry?" asked Linda.

"If you really cared about me, you would have told me," said Teressa.

"No, I could not. I had to go home with the hope that one day you will come back to me. I thought one day you and Patrick will break up and you will come home to me. What had brought you two together was no longer there. I lived with that hope until you called and told me you were pregnant again. How do you think I felt?" Linda asked with anger in her voice.

Teressa was taken aback remembering the phone call. Linda did not sound excited for her over the phone.

"Is that why you didn't sound happy?" she asked. Patrick was dumbfounded. He did not want to ask because it was clear from Linda's posture that if he asked, she was not going to respond to him and she could even stop talking and not give them the closure that they needed.

"How was I supposed to be happy for you? I cannot have kids; I have no man and the only living person that I love and care for is happy somewhere else with someone else. It was my duty to make you happy not his!" said Linda pointing at Patrick without even looking at him.

"WOW!" is all Teressa could say.

"It was my duty to make you happy," Linda repeated. "Anyway, I knew from that moment what I needed to do. I had to wait for the right time. Patrick was the problem. He has to go. Even if I get rid of this baby, he's going to make another one with you. With him gone, I will have you and the baby to myself. We can then live happily ever after," concluded Linda. She let out a large sigh after saying this. It was evident how much this secret weighed on her. Now that she had said it, she felt better.

"Are you hearing yourself Linda?" cried Teressa. "How can you think taking away what I love is going to make me happy ever after with you for all that matter?" she could not believe her ears. Teressa did not know this person in front of her.

"How long have you felt this attached to me?" she wanted to know.

"That minute you offered to pay for my school fees. I knew you were my sister for life," replied Linda.

"But you know that even sisters separate and go and marry other people. Friends are meant to be happy for each other if they are having good things in life. You were my daughter's godmother for goodness' sake," Said Teressa. She was starting to think there was something wrong with her friend.

"I wanted you to be with me all the time. Otherwise, how was I going to show you my gratitude? Anyway, why should you have everything without me?" said Linda sarcastically.

Teressa was not expecting that. "What do you mean?" She asked.

"What?" asked Patrick as well. He finally thought it was time he said something. "If you love your friend, you do not do these things to them, Linda. What type of friend are you? Are you jealous of your friend?" he asked.

"Call what you want. Call it jealousy. I call it love. I love my friend and want to be with her all the time. What I mean is that you had money, you had a rich husband, and you had a baby. You can have children. I did not have any money. I had to be taken care of by another child. I could not keep a man because I could not have children." Linda paused.

"My friend, you had it all. You even had me any time you wanted me. I saw it fit that we be together. Just you and I. One thing we have in common is that we both do not have any family of our own. So, the one we create must be mine and yours." Linda was looking at her friend saying this. Hoping to invoke some sympathy.

"You had it all too, Linda. My family was your family. It is not my fault that I had money and you did not. I shared what I had with you. How could you be so selfish?" cried Teressa.

"Not with me. You had your family with him and left me out." Said Linda still pointing at Patrick and not looking at him.

"Well, you have made sure that you lose it all. I do not want to have anything to do with you ever again. I regret the day I met you. I will sell our home and I want nothing to do with you ever. I am cutting all ties with you" said Teressa getting up and motioning to Patrick to go.

"Please don't.........." asked Linda.

"Don't what?" Teressa cut her mid-sentence.

"Do not cut me out of your life. Please forgive me. I love you, Terry. You are my one and only. You are my friend!!!!" she said shouting at Teressa as she left.

Teressa paused at the door when she heard that. She turned slowly and looked at Linda for a long hard minute.

"I am not your friend. You are my pain!!!" She shouted. "If you were my friend, you would not have caused me so much pain." She turned and left.

Linda cried. She knew from that moment that she had messed up. She did not know who to blame. She was refusing to see it all being her fault. She thought Teressa should have taken responsibility for some of her feelings.

Teressa was asking herself what type of a friend does this to another friend. They thanked Detective Brown and left. They spoke about what had happened on their way home.

"At least we now know why," said Patrick.

"We do Pat. But I feel like it has caused me more heartache than before," replied Teressa.

"What do you mean?" Patrick could not understand.

"Well, you see, when I met Linda and we became friends, I thought I had a sister that I did not have. I saw us growing old together. I saw us raising our family together. But what did she do?" asked Teressa.

"She took away the people that I love in my life. All in the name of love and friendship!" Teressa answered her own question. "Not only have I lost my baby, but I also nearly lost you, I could lose this baby too. I have also lost a best friend. A sister I never had. I have lost too much Pat. How do I cope?"

Patrick did not know how to respond. He could understand her pain. He felt some of it when they lost their baby.

"Well, at least you did not lose me. We still have this baby and more to come if you want. We have my parents. Slowly you will heal from the loss of Lisa and Linda." He tried to say what he thought would make her feel better.

"What type of a friend does that? What type of a person who moves from being a friend to being a pain! Never in a million years would I have thought my best friend could be the cause of my worst pain!" after these words from Teressa, they drove in silence until they reached home.

Teressa saw Patrick's parents' car.

"Mum and dad are here?" she said. It sounded like a question.

"Yes," said Patrick. "I thought we could do with their love at this moment"

Teressa was grateful for the thoughtfulness of her husband. She definitely needed someone she can talk to who will make sense of what she was going through. She knew that Patrick's parents were going to be there for her no matter what. They were as loving as their son.

They went into the house. Patrick's mum met them at the door and hugged Teressa really close and walked her to the lounge. Teressa cried in her arms while Patrick was telling his parents how they went and what Linda said.

"We are sorry to hear this, Terry. We love you and our love is genuine. We would never deliberately hurt you." Said Patrick's mother hugging her even closer. Patrick's father was patting her back. Teressa felt safe and loved.

Linda made a deal with the prosecution that was eventually agreed. She pleaded guilty and was sentenced without having to go through the trial process. Teressa was grateful for that. She did not want to give a witness statement. She knew the pain was going to be too much for her to relieve the last moments of her life and the moments when she thought she would lose her husband.

Linda was sentenced to life in prison. She was going to serve 30 years before she was eligible for parole. She tried to reach out to Teressa to beg her to visit her in prison and Teressa did not want to hear from her. Teressa sold their beautiful home. It felt painful for her to lose their home but it had terrible memories. Environmental health went and destroyed the poisonous plant that was around the stream.

Patrick's parents were there for them both all the time. Teressa gave birth to a baby boy. They named him Blessing. Teressa said she felt blessed to be given another chance to become a mother. Everybody was happy. They never forgot Lisa. Every year on her birthday they would visit her grave. Her brother was told about a sister he never got to meet.

Patrick planted a tree in her memory in their home. She remained a part of their lives forever. Teressa was grateful for the love around her and the family she had. Linda was becoming a memory except that at every death anniversary of Lisa, they were reminded of how she left the world and who took her. A pain of a friend as Teressa called her whenever they spoke about her.

Printed in Great Britain
by Amazon

17976207R00098